Ruin Mist 20th Anniversary

IN THE SERVICE OF DRAGONS #1

ROBERT STANEK

In the Service of Dragons #1

20th Anniversary, Signature Edition for Libraries

6th Edition, Copyright © 2020 by Robert Stanek.

Published by Big Blue Sky Press.

First Printed in the United States of America.

Book 1

Table of Contents

1

Amir, son of Ky'el, cast the orb at his feet and stepped into a spinning circle of light. "They've arrived in the high desert; the field is set. The others will come now. I only pray that all will not be lost."

"You lose faith," the other replied without looking up. "You must be patient. In the end, the paths will come together. It is so written."

"Can nothing change the course we have set upon?"

"You could no sooner catch the moon or the wind. Once set in motion, it will not stop. For now we must wait and watch. Our time will come soon enough."

"Would you have me follow them?"

"Go to the clansman, Ashwar Tae. Tell him it is time."

Amir stepped back into the spinning circle of light, disappearing and reappearing on the windswept slopes of the Rift. He appeared alongside a man on horseback and asked, "Big enough for you?" The man had the disciplined look of a soldier. He had a wide mouth, a long, sharp nose and a head of wildly unkempt copper-colored curls. He was dressed in boiled leather padded with a thick fur lining and studded with many rows of sharp steel teeth. A great sword was slung on his back and a quartet of throwing knives hung from his studded leather belt.

The man turned to grin at Amir, his few good teeth showing amongst the bad. "Indeed. It is just as you said," he declared, reaching out to grip the other's forearm. "You have kept your word, and I thank you for that."

"Don't thank me, Ashwar, thank him."

Ashwar turned back to the procession of giants, beasts, and men, thinking to himself that he'd sooner thank the Fourth himself than the King of Titans. The one was the devil he knew, the other the devil in his life—or so it seemed to him.

For hours, the two watched the procession without speaking further. The giants of the six clans lumbered by—fire and ice, storm and mountain, stone and hill. The beastmen of the Lost Lands, atop mammoths, rode by six abreast, trumpets roaring. Behind them came the Dragon Men of the Ice. Some of the Dragon Men rode great bears—black, white or brown. Others rode great wolves, either gray or white. His clansmen, the men, women and children of Oshywon, came last. Some were afoot but most were ahorse like him.

In the stories of old, Ashwar had heard of Gatherings, but he never imagined he would see one in his lifetime, let alone help to assemble it. He was excited and frightened at the same time. In the stories, Gatherings marked the end of an age and always finished badly. He wondered how this time could be any different, but he had hope. Hope was all his people clung to at times—hope for a better tomorrow, a better life, hope for a return to the plains and rivers they once knew, hope for justice and retribution, hope for their children or their children's children if not for themselves.

"Has it happened then?" he finally asked Amir.

Amir turned and knelt beside the man on horseback, staring at him eye to eye. "It has."

Ashwar cinched his horse's bridle in his hand and held him still. In the stories of old, Titans had ruled over men and elves, and Amir had the qualities of a ruler. Even with him ahorse and Amir kneeling, the Titan towered over him and it was hard to say how big he really was. Twelve feet tall maybe or fourteen, Ashwar thought, maybe taller. His broad chest and muscular arms made him seem bigger, much bigger, like some sort of towering oak that had been uprooted and transformed. But his face wasn't brutish and square like a giant's. It was refined and round, very manlike, just unusually proportioned, with a jutting chin, high cheekbones, and dark eyes so large and deep-set that they seemed high mountain caverns, or perhaps wells, whose depths swept to the Titan's very soul.

One of the giants guarding the van of the procession came upon them.

He was larger than most of the others and the fire showed clearly in his features: the long auburn-colored hair and beard, the eerie red of his eyes. He was wearing the pelt of several great bears roughly sown together and was carrying a thick spear that looked like an uprooted evergreen trimmed and sharpened yet otherwise whole. He spoke to Amir in Giantspeak and the Titan responded in kind.

"It is a good day, he says, as good a day as any," Amir told Ashwar when the giant departed.

Ashwar looked about uneasily. "A good day for what?"

"Exactly what I asked him before he hurried off to rejoin the van. Giants may be lumbering and big, but they can be hasty as well."

"Lumbering and big is an understatement."

Amir laughed as he stood—the laughter like the deep rumbling of distant thunder. "I must return. You know what must be done now?"

"I do, and I thank you for coming."

"Goodbye then, until we meet again," and so saying, Amir cast the orb at his feet and stepped into the spinning circle of light.

As he emerged from shadow, Amir found Noman playing at Destiny Sticks. He went to a window without saying a word but it was not the view beyond that he was interested in—it was Noman. Seated with a hunch-backed posture, Noman seemed a small man; yet standing with his shoulders back and straight, he seemed regal. Amir didn't know whether it was the veins of black that streaked otherwise pure white hair, the eyebrows with matching spikes of black mixed with gray or the beard that flowed to the middle of his chest in a sheet of pure silver that made Noman seem a king, but he seemed a king nonetheless—and a great king at that. But Noman was not a king; he was but a man who lived among Titans in the City of the Sky.

"It seems so futile, this waiting," Amir complained.

Noman cast the sticks upon the table, looking up momentarily to regard the other. In girth, Amir's shoulders spread from one side of the grand window to the other, filling its opening when he turned his back to the light. "And when the wait is over, what then?"

Amir didn't answer. Instead he watched as Noman played at the game of Destiny, carefully picking out the black and white sticks representing the Path, avoiding the gray sticks of the Void. Lost in the rhythm of the game, his thoughts soon carried him into the distant past.

"Are we then outside time?" a much younger Amir asked the figure in his mind's eye.

"Time affects all things, even those who consider themselves outside its grasp."

"But why me? Why me when there were so many others more deserving?"

"It is as it must be."

"But I have done nothing to receive so great an honor."

"That is untrue. You were the most skilled of your kind ever to walk the earth."

"You talk in the past; am I not dead then?"

Noman smiled. "Back to the same question. Your thoughts move in circles. You know you are not. The Father has true need of your skills when the time is right."

While in the waking world Noman's hands busily worked the sticks, Amir's thoughts slipped further into the past. To his right, Antwar Alder, the man who would be king, swept Truth Bringer from its sheath, the great blade seeming to outshine the moon with its own inner light and lending a pale shadow over the strong-faced Antwar.

Ky'el touched his arm. "Ready yourself, son."

An adolescent Amir nodded. "I swore an oath, a holy oath I mean to keep."

"There are more," whispered Etry. "Where are Aven and Riven?"

Amir looked down the line. The city's outer defenses had failed and the last of the defenders made their stand at the Greye, the very keep built by their enemy Dnyarr. Across Gregortonn's High Square the first charge of the night began with the cracks of whips from the goblin lieutenants sending the dog packs into a frenzied, howling run. The lines of human slaves followed; and behind them came the chariots of the elves pulled by the black, wingless dragons of the Samguinne.

Ky'el thundered toward the line, his silver cloak streaming from his shoulders. Amir tried to follow.

Dust seemed to be blowing everywhere. Keeping up with the shadowy figure charging into the battle required his full attention.

The besiegers began screaming and cheering as the packs set into the lines, their screams and cheers in stark contrast to the cries of pain from the defenders, the sound of it all very nearly blocking out the strange whistling from above. By the time Amir saw the first black-feathered arrow strike one of his fellows, it was too late.

An arrow hit him full in the chest, piercing his breastplate. An instant later, he found himself on the other side. "Am I dead or am I dreaming?" he asked himself as he floated in the void.

"Not dead," said the voice from out of the void—the voice Amir would in later years come to know as Noman's. "Your path continues far beyond this place."

"Where am I? Why am I here?"

"Ky'el's time comes to an end. *Look*, the arrow has pierced his heart, not yours." It was the first use of the compelling voice Amir had encountered and it was in that moment that he realized he was cradling Ky'el—that the arrow had pierced Ky'el's armor not his own.

Hot tears streamed down his cheeks. The battle was all but over.

"What am I to do?"

"You shall find out soon. Now is not the time."

"What is this place?"

"The world of dreams and reality are closely knit, very closely knit," Noman said. "Ofttimes the two appear as one and the same, or perhaps another. Some exist in a state of perpetual dream, others in a state of eternal life, and a few in a state of the dream within their eternal life. You, my young friend, find the dream at a time when life's need is at its greatest."

Amir was halfway through a response when he realized he was back in the present, sitting in the great window with the fading sun casting his shadow long upon the floor. Hours had passed. Noman had laid out the final path upon the table. "Is it what I—?" he started to ask but was interrupted.

"Must you always dwell in the past?" Noman asked.

"There, you see, even when I think, I cannot be alone."

"That is as it must be. Come, even you must eat. Ah, and before you complain, this is what you wanted. I know it is."

Amir looked at the food spread out in front of him like a feast. "Yes, but I changed my mind."

"No you didn't. You shouldn't fool with an old man's mind."

"An old man? You are the one who taught me that appearance is meaningless."

Noman's eyes flashed. "Appearance is everything; you would do well to remember that."

Amir made no further comment and instead ate until he was content then walked back to his window to continue his watch. Time passed without change. As Noman stared at the Destiny Sticks and busily consulted his books, Amir waited in silence as the sun disappeared over the horizon.

The next day brought more restlessness. Amir paced back and forth, occasionally glancing out the window. Both he and Noman could sense a change, a presence that could not be explained in words. Noman didn't show his anxiety as much as Amir did although within he was indeed anxious. He could sense it just as much as Amir could.

Seeking to ease the tension, Noman began to concentrate, focusing his thoughts, cycling the Magicks through his body discreetly. His hope was to catch Amir off guard; but after centuries of being with Noman, Amir responded to the attack with catlike grace, unsheathing his goliath, double-edged bastard sword, turning, lifting, and striking out at his invisible opponent in the time it took most to inhale a single breath.

The resonant clang of metal striking metal soon filled the air. Amir knew his opposition well; after all, it was himself. He fought his own shadow as always and it knew his every move, his every trick. It remembered each time that Amir had overcome it in the past. It fed on those defeats so that each time Amir was forced to think differently or to act differently, thus improving his performance or making him stronger and faster so he could defeat it.

He charged repeatedly, wielding his weapon with the ease and skill of a master, the generous weight of its mass carefully balanced in his hands. He attempted a simple combination, thrust, parry, thrust, followed quickly by a thrust, slice, and a feint. The shadow seemed to mock him as it followed his every move and counter.

"Will I ever be able to fight this beast in reality?" Amir asked, gritting his teeth, circling left.

"Concentrate," Noman responded, "Concentrate or you will become the shadow."

Amir dropped, rolled and thrust upward with his blade. The shadow blocked and circled.

"It seems so fruitless, all this training, all this waiting. What will happen then, afterward?"

Noman raised his eyebrows, sensing the intent in the words. "Do not fret so. The day comes, revel in that, but trust me when I say you will wish it hadn't."

Through the afternoon the assault continued. Amir's blade broke the air about him wildly, pushing the shadow into a corner. He was nearly winded but he couldn't let his fatigue show. The shadow had an advantage over him. It never tired, it was relentless, it learned with every breath. So even as Amir moved in for the kill, the shadow countered and waited for the lunge that was meant to end its existence; then it cackled in delight.

As Amir's blade met empty air, he shouted, "This is going nowhere!"

"Your mind is overly occupied elsewhere. You should not be thinking of Ashwar and the clansmen! Focus upon what is important!"

"Concentrate, concentrate," Amir exhorted himself. Nearing exhaustion, his only resource left was a gambit. He jumped into the air. Midway through a forward somersault, he struck down, only to slice empty air.

He landed, recovered from the momentary surprise, dodged a well-timed blow from the shadow, spun, and then hurled his sword outward. This time his blade struck true and the creature roared its defeat. The shadow had done exactly what Amir expected it to do. It had dodged his first attack and tried to attack him from behind as he landed. The next sweep of the creature's blade should have caught him except that Amir spun to the right instead of to the left where the shadow had been; and as it countered, Amir struck outward with the lethal blow, ending the match in victory as always.

Sweat glistening from his muscular body, Amir sheathed his sword and wiped perspiration from his brow. He was tired, very tired, though he would not show it. He had learned from the shadow as much as it had learned from him and he would not forget the lesson. Steadying himself, he returned to the great window and his vigil.

That evening the two supped in silence, lost in thought. As the last light of the day gave way to the darkness of the night, Noman looked up from his books. "You must be patient. Watch, but take no action." His guarded expression said everything. The hour had come; the long wait was over. Amir cast the orb at his feet, but before he could step into the spinning circle of light, Noman spoke again. "Heed my warning, take no action. Watch, and when it is over, return to report."

Amir stepped into the circle of light, disappearing and reappearing on the desolate sands of the Barrens. The air in the high mountain desert was chill and growing colder by the moment as the wind sucked the warmth of the day from the sand. In the distance he could see a bonfire, its dull orange glow a beacon in the darkness. Two figures moved around the fire; but it was the third, lying in sleep, that interested him the most. He called out a challenge to the wind and waited.

2

Competing with the northeasterly wind, a hunter's call of greeting came, and the Eagle Lord cocked his head a full half circle as only a bird or a birdman could do. In other times he would have returned the call but not this night. The yearning faded quickly; and the blue eyes that were those of a man, not those of a bird, returned their focus to the soft, low fire where the two sat.

"They are restless," whispered Ayrian, his beak-like mouth clicking with each word. "They call to calm the air beneath them as well as their own fear for their hunts."

Xith turned earnest eyes to the north, wanting to see and hear what the Eagle Lord saw, yet even his eyes—eyes that could see in the dark and were the color of pale moonlight—could see only the darkness. As he stood staring, gusts of wind whipped his cloak to his back, wrapped the black wool around his short stubby legs, then furled it out behind him. He replied, "There is always a trade-off to be made. Why should it be any different at this late hour?"

Ayrian fixed his gaze into the night sky, craning his neck at an angle no man could achieve. "Father Wind can sense it as well."

Xith stretched the stiffness from his legs and wriggled his toes to get his blood circulating. For a moment, he wondered if his wondrous companion could truly sense the will of the wind and an odd smile came to his lips, exaggerated by the thick wrinkles of his timeworn face. He wondered also if Ayrian could sense the tainted will of the Fourth closing in all around them. He *could*.

Not much else was said as the night passed slowly. The hours of darkness and solitude gave both the watcher and the great lord time for reflection; for Xith it was a time to contemplate tomorrow, for Ayrian it was a time to reflect on the past.

The wind, which had blown unsteadily throughout the night, changed directions with the coming of the day, blowing from the north as if to remind the two of what was ahead. They turned in unison to look on Vilmos as he stirred in his sleep.

Xith asked, "Will you be able to do what I cannot if it is so?"

"I will do what must needs be done." Ayrian looked to Vilmos, his face an expressionless mask. "For what other reason would you have wanted me here?"

Xith reached out, gripped Ayrian's arm above the elbow. "I did not expect otherwise but I needed to hear it, old friend."

The sun was already full in the sky when Vilmos awoke after what seemed to him an endless sleep. In his mind's eye, he could still see

Adrina's tears, his last image before sleeping. Yet he was not saddened by her betrayal. Instead, he was numb, as if he could no longer feel; and the fire beside him did not warm him.

He absently brushed his thick black hair away from his brown eyes, thinking of Lillath and what she'd say if she saw him looking such a mess. The thought was fleeting, however, and he began to wonder if he were in another dream, a dream like the others he'd experienced before.

He heard muddled words yet didn't understand them. It took an effort to drive the final wisps of sleep from his eyes and rise to a seated position, but he persevered. He worked the kinks out of his neck with gentle twists and craning motions then stretched to ease the pain in his back. He tried to stand. Unsteady limbs would not allow him to get much farther than his knees, and it was from this uncanny half crawl, half stand that he turned bleary eyes toward his companions.

The sight of Ayrian startled him at first. The Eagle Lord faced the sun with his hands cupped and outstretched in the air in front of him. Ayrian sang, words whose sounds blurred together and seemed to be but a single extended word. Vilmos listened inattentively at first; then, drawn in by the rhythm, he could think of nothing else. His body swayed to the measure of the fleeting echoes of the song. He forgot the pain, forgot that he was on his knees, and forgot the dreams of the night past. He knew only the rhythm of the song as it swept over him, the sounds floating to his ears as if borne upon the air by wings unseen.

His mind wandered within the melody. A part of him recognized the song though he couldn't quite grasp its meaning. For a moment it seemed the world was without time, but time did not stop. The sun climbed to its zenith. Clouds came and went; the wind blew; and the song continued.

Vilmos felt he was living a dream. He watched Ayrian's shadow step away from his body and turn about. He raised his hands in alarm as if that could ward off the shadow, but Ayrian seemed not to notice the shadow at all.

The shadow continued, touching his face to the ground, kissing the earth and weeping openly with joy. And it was only as he righted himself that the shadow Ayrian seemed to notice Vilmos at all.

Vilmos spoke first. "What is happening?" he asked. The shadow Ayrian said not a word. He studied Vilmos as if seeing a thing strange to his eyes. Vilmos whispered, "This place, I know it."

The shadow Ayrian reached out and as his fingertips pressed against Vilmos' cheek, reality folded in on shadow and Vilmos was left staring up at the real Ayrian.

Ayrian looked down at Vilmos with his hand extended. Vilmos hesitated then accepted the hand, allowing Ayrian to pull him to his feet. Vilmos heard himself ask, "Do we journey now, Ayrian, Lord of the Gray Clan?" But it was not his voice that filled his ears.

Vilmos continued to stare, confused. Ayrian steadied him so that he did not fall. He tried to speak again but no words came.

"It will pass," Ayrian said, "give yourself a moment. The strength will return and the voices will fade."

"Xith, where's Xith?"

"You are in the company of friends. Do not worry."

"Am I?" Vilmos asked. Ayrian touched the medallion that was suspended from Vilmos' neck by a thick gold chain, and Vilmos seemed to feel its weight for the first time.

"The Magicks no longer have dominion over you. You are free."

Memories of priests, a warrior, and fighting came flooding behind his eyes. Vilmos saw blood everywhere. He heard screams. He staggered and went to his knees but Ayrian kept him from completely collapsing under his own weight. "Am I truly free?"

"You are confused. Trust your instincts. Your mind will clear."

Vilmos, beyond confusion, found himself at a total loss for words though he tried to respond. He stammered, paused. His eyes went wide. "The door has been opened! Beware that the Darkess return!"

"Old friend, do not fight it. These are but memories. Dnyarr and Alexia are no more. The bastards Riven and Aven are gone with them and the dark past. Accept that the memories are your own. You have only to unite the old with the new."

A barrier seemed to break in the back of Vilmos' mind; another's thoughts came flooding inward, overwhelming him. He once again spoke with the other's voice. "Shall we then find my beloved? Is it yet time?"

"The day has not come; she rests and longs for the day you will join her."

A distant flash of lightning followed by a clap of thunder caught Vilmos by surprise. Ayrian turned and smelled the air as if sensing something. Vilmos wondered if perhaps the Eagle Lord could smell the storm and the rain that was surely coming their way, but he wasn't able to dwell on the thought for long before his mind succumbed to the turmoil of the voice within.

As the voice grew, so did his hunger, a hunger beyond the normal complaints of his empty stomach. It grew from the deepest reaches within, extending through to his very soul. It ate at the edges of the blackness that were the corners of his will; and as he struggled, time passed.

Night seemed to arrive suddenly, dark and overcast. The wind picked up as the storm raged nearby, and then came the rain, seemingly gentle at first, perhaps soothing, but not for long. The earth beneath his feet soon turned to mud as waters swelled all around him, nearly washing away the camp, and it was all he could do to hold his own against the wind and the rain.

The air grew cold as if warmth were being sucked out by an unseen force. Brilliant flashes of white lightning danced all around him. "Ayrian? Xith?" he called out.

No one answered. Vilmos huddled down, hugging his knees to stay warm. Dark thoughts came. The voice of his dreams, his nightmares, found him. Fatigue swept over him and when he could no longer hold his eyes open, he fell into a deep sleep and it was then that the struggle for self began.

Ayrian and Xith stepped from the shadows. It was Xith who knelt beside Vilmos to check his breathing, and Xith who cast an enchantment to ensure the boy's sleep would not be disturbed.

"Is it come to pass?" Ayrian asked.

"I have seen the point at which the paths split but only the passing of the hour will decide it, as ever."

Sensing something unseen, Ayrian twisted his head around to look behind them. He sensed the others then and started to cry out, "It begins," but it was too late. The dark kin were already sweeping in from all sides, bringing with them a true darkness that fell upon them unlike any other. And in this darkness, death walked with the shades of the night, striking blows that could not be dodged or seen.

Xith slumped to the ground as a raking blow struck cleanly and harshly. Pain and surprise made him scream out and curse the darkness, but he cast a pledge along with his curse as he regained his feet. He vowed that he would not submit to their touch this night or any other. Death by touch of the kin was not a clean death, for it meant damnation. His soul would not journey to the Father and would instead serve the powers of darkness until they had drunk of its goodness and turned it into the very thing that had delivered its destruction.

The Eagle Lord looked on, vying for his own freedom, struggling to break past the horde of attackers. He backed away, great wings raised, revealing his razor sharp claws, and for a brief moment the dark kin were hesitant to descend upon him; also in that same brief moment the strengths of the two defenders were revealed.

Ayrian took flight, using his powerful wings to cut into the air. Xith called balls of lightning to his hands as a swarm of shadowy shapes surrounded him. The disorientation from the swift attacks eased from their minds, yet little by little they were corralled into a close-knit circle formed by the black beasts. In the air, Ayrian contended with dark kin that rode on the backs of shadow dragons. On the ground, Xith defended against those who marshaled shadow hounds before them and some who rode upon winged chargers wrapped in shadow.

Xith stepped protectively over Vilmos, yelling, "Beware the touch!" His strong constitution enabled him to recover readily from the life-draining touch but he feared for Ayrian. There was evident weakness in the Eagle Lord's movements and the creatures knew this. It excited them—a new soul, a powerful soul, would bring great reward.

Ayrian poured his reserve strength into his powerful wings, trying to rise above the attackers, yet he was beaten back again and again. Seeing this, Xith dodged the razor claws about him, gradually drawing energy inside him. He knew these creatures well; dark kin were to be feared greatly by mortal men, yet he was not a mere mortal, and he would not be intimidated by sheer numbers alone. He called to the earth and the earth rumbled and shook at his call. Then, raising his arms, he brought forth the stone of the earth, sending earth and rock flying outward and upward into the dark land and sky.

Ayrian shot up into the heavens, then whirled about to face the enemies about him. Many of the kin were taken by surprise, and he used the temporary advantage to dispatch several before they came at him again with renewed hate. As he was dodging in and out of their reaching blows, he noticed the creature about to lunge upon Xith from behind. With no hesitation and no second thoughts, he tucked his wings to his side and plunged from the skies to Xith's aid, striking the kin, knocking it to the ground, as well as himself. He lay there motionless as the dark kin faced him, his demeanor silently telling Xith he was playing decoy and that Xith should go about his own retaliations.

Ayrian's eyes glowed as wild magic surged through him, and it was in the instant when the dark kin set upon him that he unleashed his shadow self. The shadow Ayrian caught the unsuspecting kin off guard, his blows causing a searing white light to issue forth wherever he scored a hit as the creature's soul sought release from its capture. In the end, the dying kin could only cry out into the storm-swept sky, a plea to its dark master that most certainly went unanswered.

Xith whipped around to face a beast at his left just as it struck him. He was still reeling under the weight of the heavy blow when Ayrian, who had defeated the only creature that lay between him and the shaman, drummed the dark kin with a deadly blow. In a flash of light, the dark kin disappeared.

Wearily, Xith stood, steadying himself as the momentary confusion waned. Ayrian hovered to his immediate left, using steady strokes of his great wings to shoulder his bulk while he waited for the next wave.

Finally the energy within Xith reached its crescendo and shortly after it peaked he released it, unleashing it in a wide arc before him as waves of rose-pink light. The dark kin, struck by the arcing waves, were engulfed and enshrouded in shimmering silver silhouettes from which they could not escape, and one by one they vanished in a bright white blink of light.

Hesitant, the last few dark kin regrouped and came in for another attack. Blood ran from where Xith was gouged and raked; still he would not give in. Again he drank in the energies of the land, devouring its forces and reshaping them to his own desires, trusting Ayrian would be able to delay the onslaught while he was vulnerable to their attack. Ayrian, for his part, slashed and hacked, wildly directing every ounce of his remaining strength, as the dark kin swept in.

Xith waited to the last, feinted to the right, then rolled to the ground. He spun around with awe-inspiring swiftness, his face aglow, his hands, raised high, enveloped in wild, uncontained magic; but the arc of lightning shot wide, missed its mark, and faded away useless. Without pause, he lashed out again—a release less powerful than he had hoped for but effective all the same. A slow tracing of energy encircled two dark kin and the winged shadow-dragons they rode upon. Death reclaimed the beasts. Death to such creatures was defeat, measured in torment, and delivered by their dark masters.

With the odds more in their favor, Ayrian sprang headlong into the remaining group while Xith charged fearlessly. These powerful two against the remaining six was little contest, yet the dark kin did not see things through the eyes of their enemies. Ayrian parried several attempts to force him back, striking one of the dark kin with a clean blow that should have ended its pitiful, tormented existence, yet did not. And it was as he was struggling under the beasts' counterattacks that Ayrian sensed a force in these remaining creatures that he had not perceived in the others. His next blow, a well-placed strike to the midsection, did end the wounded beast's life, but only a moment before it would have struck him with a potentially lethal blow.

Xith, preoccupied with maintaining the magic within him and shaping his next attack, did not notice what Ayrian had discovered. He was near exhaustion, and he had no doubt that Ayrian was near exhaustion as well. His aim was to deliver a blow that would end the fray before it was too late for one or all of them, and so he called upon the powers of life and death, forces in opposition with each other and the natural order, allowing magic, chaste and powerful, to come to him, yearning to be released. To create the positive force of life, Xith had to balance the negative force of death—the very power from which the dark kin were created—as well, and it was a very fine balance indeed. One misstep would mean his own life, and possibly that of Vilmos whom he stood over. But he preferred a quick death to what the dark kin would bring to him—and to Vilmos—if he failed.

For a moment, his resolve faded as fatigue swept over him. "Please forgive me, Great Father," he shouted as sparks of intertwined rose-pink and blue-white light illuminated the dark sky, arcing from his outstretched hands to sweep over the five remaining dark kin. The powers in opposition were so overwhelming as they clashed that the backlash knocked Xith to the ground and swept Ayrian away into the darkness of the night.

Xith struggled to stand, hoping for the end but finding instead that one of the dark kin remained. In that moment, it would have been so easy to give in to fatigue. He had only to pause, to let his knees buckle, to drop where he stood and succumb. It is what a little voice in the back of his mind urged him to do; it is what he wanted to do. But he couldn't ignore the other little voice in the back of his mind asking him about Vilmos and Ayrian and their fate should he give in. It was that voice that kept him on his feet when he would otherwise have succumbed to his wounds and to exhaustion.

The dark creature did not try to flee; it welcomed its return to the darkness it had sprung from and wanted only to taste sweet revenge. It seized the opportunity as Xith struggled to pounce. But it did not go after the magic-wielder; it went after Ayrian, trying to claim that which it felt was due, Ayrian's soul. The blow it delivered was skillfully placed, up through the rib cage, direct to the beating heart, and as its icy razor-like claws sliced inward and upward, Ayrian countered, but it was too late. Both fell where they were as death sought to embrace them.

The dark creature gripped Ayrian's heart. Its success seemed assured and it cried in glee. But glee turned to despair and then to anguish as an unseen force ripped it back and away. As the dark kin faded from sight, Xith collapsed at Vilmos' side. The raw magic of life itself caressed his outstretched hands momentarily before winking out. The battle was over, but what had it cost? Ayrian was near death. Xith was battered and bruised, his long dark cloak tattered and saturated with his own blood. And Vilmos lay still, trapped in his dreams, unaware that the first battle for his future and that of all the kingdoms of men and elves alike had been fought.

The multiple wounds spoke silently of heroic deeds, for with each touch the raw energies of life had been sucked from Xith's limbs, and yet he persisted and resisted the call of death. As for the vanquished foes, there were no hints or traces that said they ever existed or that the valiant two had defeated the many; the scene only revealed that a struggle had taken place and that while one was near death, lying in an ever expanding pool whose hue was reflected as ebony by the night sky, one lived.

Xith knelt beside his fallen friend and heedless of his own weakening will, he began the healing and binding magic. His skills as a healer were limited; he could bind the smaller wounds and slow the bleeding of the largest; otherwise, he could not aid in the healing process. He considered the days and nights ahead with dread, through which he would have to maintain a vigilant watch if Ayrian were to survive.

Pushing dark thoughts aside he focused; and as the last of the magic spilled from his hands, the last of his will slipping with it, he passed from consciousness for a time, not noticing the shrouded figure that approached him and touched a hand, palm down, to his brow, bidding him to find calm in his sleep. And sleep he did, seemingly outside of time.

In the shadows of his mind, he thought he saw the arrival of day as a pink haze before his closed lids, but when he awoke it was dark and night reigned. The sky had cleared and bright stars shown down upon the campsite, outlining the silhouette of a shrouded figure that still stood over him, bent downward away from the starlit night so that deep shadows played across the hidden face.

The figure beckoned Xith to sit and as the dark form turned to face the night sky, the shaman glimpsed the contours of the face. He could almost recognize the widely set brow and the distinctive curve of the nose, yet there was something peculiar about the mysterious figure. He leaned in for closer inspection and was taking note of the subtle changes when the figure suddenly vanished.

A voice replaced the dark shape; a voice that startled Xith and seemed so distant. "Hello, Xith," the voice playfully stated.

"Does this remind you of something?" The voice became but a fading echo in Xith's mind. He turned a full circle to find only empty air.

He blamed his confusion on the battle, telling himself that the effects of the heavy battle still played on his mind. He was drained and tired. He wasn't thinking clearly, and his body was too sore and slow to respond.

"Can you stop my wind?" begged the other.

The wind, which had been a gentle breeze a moment before, blew with tempest force. Xith did not falter in the face of it, nor did he try to stop it. He maintained his footing, standing motionless with his eyes closed, focusing his thoughts on his center, cleansing his mind, clearing his will. When he was ready he spoke, simply and eloquently, saying, "So the teacher becomes the pupil and the pupil becomes the teacher. Welcome home Wanderer!"

"I am not he," Vilmos said as he appeared before Xith.

Xith was not startled by that fact, yet he was troubled by the changes that were occurring in Vilmos. "I must tend to Ayrian. He must be one of our company, for I have seen the path's end without him."

"He will sleep," was all Vilmos said, as he provoked the wind on.

Xith returned to the spot where Ayrian lay. He touched a hand to the eagle lord's forehead, bringing it down the line of the neck to the chest. "What have you done?" He paused then added, using the commanding nature of the Voice, "*Release him* at once; it is my wish and my will."

"He will sleep and when he awakes he will know nothing of the pain. The wounds will be gone; they are gone. Can you not see?"

Xith moved toward Vilmos. It was clear that a struggle was taking place within or had already taken place and was troubling the boy's thoughts. Xith wondered who had survived within Vilmos and of the boy's intentions.

"Who am I? Who am I? Do you really want to know?" asked Vilmos, laughing into the night sky. "I am he who survived. I am he who has overcome." The strength faded from his words as he spoke, his voice cracked "I am he that is left." The last was spoken in a whisper and the wind ceased, leaving the former teacher and the former pupil facing each other.

Xith's fears eased as he stared into now familiar eyes. He felt like the father whose son has just returned to him; and when boyish features returned to the stern face, the shaman wholeheartedly embraced Vilmos. "I must tend to Ayrian and then we must cross the desert and climb the mountain, a fitting beginning to a long journey along a dark road through hidden realms."

"I know," Vilmos said, and the other voice whispered before it dwindled and died, "To the cloud city at last where we will join the dwellers of the sky."

Xith put his hands on the boy's shoulders and nodded solemnly. The Wanderer, who had outlived the whole of his brethren and had witnessed the births and deaths of races and of nations, had come home at last, if only in the form of the boy before him. Vilmos would be bound forever and inexorably to memories of things as ancient as the wind and to the Wanderer, who was now a part of him.

Unseen in the distance, Ky'el nodded satisfaction and returned via the orb to the City of the Sky.

3

The nearby garrison at Imtal was the first stop of many and the days of journey afterward came and went uneventfully and unremarkably, giving Seth time to reflect. His thoughts drifted mostly to the past, only moving from his reveries to the present momentarily when Valam pointed out sites of interest; and then he would slip back into a near yet distant place.

Valam for his part hoped they would see some action. Many of the men they traveled with were untested, green if truth be told, and a clean, decisive victory on the open road would go a long way toward easing the men's worries about what was ahead—worries that Valam shared yet did not voice. But such hopes weren't meant to be. Even the bandits who pillaged deep into the kingdom weren't brazen enough to attack a group as large as the entourage he traveled with, and so the days slowly continued one after the other.

Valam's only pleasures were the lightly salted and heavily smoked venison in his saddlebag and the mead he shared with the men after evenfall. Without the venison to chew on during the day and the drink to ease him to sleep after a long day in the saddle, the journey would have seemed unbearably long.

At times, Valam thought of the elf Galan and how she had sacrificed herself to save Seth. He wondered if he would have done the same for his sister Adrina or another. Somehow he didn't think he would have—not that he was afraid to die, death he wasn't afraid of—more that he wasn't sure the trade off Galan had made was a wise one. *Why her and not him?* That was the question that gnawed at him during the day and troubled his dreams as he slept. It was an issue that had come between him and Seth to the detriment of their friendship, but it did not dissuade his resolve. He knew what was ahead; with his own eyes he had seen war sweep the land, and just as important, he believed what he had seen. Now was a time for action and on that his resolve did not waver, despite the thinking of some on his father's council—and perhaps his father himself. As he guided his black charger along the road, he struggled with the thought of what his betrayal would mean to Seth. *Would Seth understand? Would he even be able to do what his father asked of him?*

At King's Crossing where the East-West and North-South roads met, the group decided to bypass the lowland marshes of Fraddylwicke, electing to take the longer, more reliable route along the East-West road to the coast. Such a turning brought the group to the Barony of Klaive, where the baron and his sons gave the prince and men a great feast such as many of the men had never known. After Klaive, the group passed through the free cities at the mouth of River Trollbridge. The Trollbridge, unlike its sister in the North, the Krasnyj, which flowed only sporadically throughout the year and stretched nearly from sea to sea, flowed all year with but a single purpose: to inundate the Bottoms. The history of the Trollbridge and the Bottoms was older than that of Great

Kingdom, stretching far into the past now unknown, but that history paled when compared to that of Mir and Veter, the free cities themselves. It was true that the Kingdom Alliance kept the cities free, but it was also true that the alliance had been bought with blood. There was a saying of old in the free cities: "of candor and liberty I know much, of justice and sincerity I know little." For many it was true and the last words they spoke before their lives were bought with blood.

A day after passing through the free cities, the group camped on the northern edge of the Belyj, a forest Valam knew better than the city of Imtal where he had grown up, a forest that was his own. And here he breathed easier than he had in days—in truth, since the journey had begun. Somehow the air in South Province felt better as he breathed it in. He couldn't explain why, but perhaps it was the heavy scent of ash, elm and birch mixed in with the remnants of the salt spray from the distant West Deep. Earth and summer trees, salt and water, this was the smell of his home, the home he had made for himself over the past five years— years that had been lean and tough but years during which he had grown into the man he was today.

From the Belyj, it was a few days' journey to Quashan' the capital of South Province and their destination, but before then, he aimed to test Seth and the bonds of their friendship. It was a thing he had promised himself that he would do, but now that the hour of the deed was nearing, he had doubts. *Could he lessen the sting of what he must do?* Seth had proven himself true in Quashan' and in Imtal; his brethren had sacrificed everything to gain an audience with Valam's father, King Andrew Alder;

and the Queen Mother had opened everyone's eyes to truth. And he himself had knelt before his father, promising his sword to the elves' cause. He had promised Adrina that he would hold true to his word, and he had ridden from Imtal with a force ten thousand strong—soldiers, hired blades, and tradesmen all. *So why did he have lingering doubts? Why had he made himself promise such a thing? And why did such a thing have to be?*

He pushed the thoughts from his mind, put his heels into his surefooted charger, and flew. One of the hunting dogs raced along beside him, with its tail held high, its gray fur ruffed up thick against the passing rain. The other dogs followed; and somewhere behind them in the long line of horses and men were Captain Vadan Evgej, the hunt master with his ready bow and horn, and Seth ahorse a dapple gray courser.

Valam entered the sanctuary of the forest without hesitation, the canopy of the trees breaking the rainfall. Soon he could hear only the sound of hooves and paws and faintly, the rain. He remembered how he'd felt the first time he hunted: nervous as a raw recruit to the king's guard, but eager for the hunt. *Well, here's to the hunt,* he told himself as he turned the charger down an overgrown game trail. In the back of his mind, he could hear Father Jacob cursing because he, Prince of Great Kingdom and Lord of the South, was at the front of the hunting party and not safely in its midst; and he laughed aloud to himself, his voice echoing off the trees and mixing with the crunching of leaves.

The air was cool and Valam cursed himself for not wearing a thicker cloak or discarding the wet one now clinging to his back. But he didn't want to waste a moment; and as he broke into a clearing, he was glad he hadn't waited for the others. He took up the bow from his shoulder, notched an arrow, and was ready to draw. A twelve-point stag was straight across from him in the clearing, looking on, seemingly unafraid.

He touched the nock of the arrow, drew to his cheek in one swift movement but didn't release. Instead he held the bowstring as he stared into the black eyes of the stag. It wasn't often one met a Prince of Stags; and the stag, for his part, lifted his head high and stared back at Valam unafraid.

For a time Valam waited, a prince of the city studying a worthy prince of the forest. He shifted his bow irritably to rub at his arms and told himself to release the bowstring but found that he could not. He glanced over his shoulder, looking back down the overgrown trail but found that the others hadn't made the turn, or at least it didn't seem so, for he was alone with the stag. Well, nearly so. The gray bitch was beside his charger; she didn't make a move either.

It was more habit than anything else that kept the bow in his hands and the string drawn. The thick muscles of his arms tensed and rippled, but such effort was not unknown to him. As a boy his father's master trainer had made him hold poses for hours with a great sword, a pike, a battle ax, or whatever else was the weapon of choice that day. He had learned to endure the strain and the inevitable cramps. The master's training had also helped him to learn to see what could otherwise go unseen.

Taking in more of the clearing, he saw that not more than ten paces behind the stag was a large doe and a pair of summer fawns. The doe was afraid, for she seemed to be shivering as Valam set his eyes on her. He shivered too, but only from the cold. His rider's cloak covered him to his boot tips; the cowl was pulled back, however, and the rain soaked him as it streamed through the opening in the forest canopy.

He managed a weak smile. Of all the things he could have thought about right then, it was Adrina, his sister, who was probably warm and dry in her night chambers, who came to mind. He wondered what she would think of the irony of such a scene: himself with an arrow nocked and drawn, the stag, the doe and the fawns waiting.

His eyes on the stag now seemed to be playing a trick on him, for instead of an animal, he saw a man clad in dapple gray almost the color of Seth's courser. He blinked. In the stag's place was Seth and beside him, the hunt master.

"My lord prince," Evgej called out to him, seeming ill at ease with Valam's bow drawn and aimed at him. "We had thought you lost."

Valam lowered the bow and returned the arrow to the quiver. He decided to say nothing of the stag, and instead called back, "It is an honor to hunt with your hunters this evening, captain."

"The honor is all mine," Captain Vadan Evgej called back, signaling to the others to cross the clearing to the prince.

Seth touched Valam's mind with a thought—the method he was using to teach Valam and others who were willing to listen—that their thoughts were open and thus readable. Valam responded instinctively by clouding his thoughts as he had been taught, effectively blocking his thoughts so they couldn't be read. It was an automatic response as taught by Seth, but he also did not need any more confusion. For the past few days Seth's presence had put him increasingly on edge whenever they were together. Worse, Seth seemed to be aware of it but hadn't said anything about it.

He was hoping Seth had not noticed his unease when Seth said, "This is my first hunt. I am not sure what to do."

Valam smiled but didn't say anything immediately. He was focused on the men crossing the clearing. "The hunt is easy. You must only ride along. I do not expect you to make a kill. I know it is not your way."

"As do I," Evgej said, his shiny wet leather jerkin dripping as he turned in beside Valam.

Valam studied the tall, lanky hunt master. Evgej didn't wear a hat and the rain matted his fair hair. A bushy yellow beard hid most of his face, and a silver hunting horn was slung over his right shoulder. On his back was a longbow, a quiver with arrows fletched in white goose feathers, and a wine bag. By all appearances Evgej was early into his middle years, but Valam knew that the semblance of age was only an illusion. Evgej was no older than he, just over twenty.

"We hunt for food as much as for sport," Valam said turning to Seth.

The elf pushed back the hood of his cloak; his blue eyes seemingly drank in Valam's soul. If Valam hadn't known Seth was elf kin, he might have thought him kin of Evgej. The hair and the lithe limbs said both were fair folk of the summer forest. Seth, however, seemed untouched by the rain. It was as if the rain danced around him. His deep burgundy cloak appeared to be dry and his medium-length hair was untouched, even that which hadn't been protected by the cowl. "You need not worry about me. I understand the need for a hunt as much as any other."

"Shall we continue then, my lord?" Evgej asked. Valam nodded agreement. Evgej turned to his huntsmen, shouting, "Let the hunt continue!" as he directed their attentions back to the hunt. He sent his men out ahead to circle in front and flush the game toward the clearing. As they did so, he strung his finely crafted oaken longbow and waited. He indicated that Seth and Valam should ready themselves, yet only Valam notched an arrow and waited.

As the sound of the chasers drew nearer, the woods around them came to life. Birds burst into the air flapping on frantic wings and rabbits darted to and fro, but it was the stag that caught Evgej's eye first. As the large animal made its way readily into the clearing, Evgej offered the first flight to Valam. Valam didn't hesitate; his arrow took the stag between the neck and shoulder, a near perfect shot but not fatal.

The stag stumbled, snorted in pain and twisted its head as if to use its small rack to ward off the distant attackers. Evgej aimed, released. His shot, perfect and deadly, dropped the stag where it stood. It was an impressive shot to be sure, especially considering the angle Evgej had released from.

Robert Stanek

The sun was beginning to set and the day was getting dark, but the rain had passed for the most part. The hunt master's steward, a broad-shouldered boy with wavy chestnut hair and a constellation of freckles, dismounted and made ready to retrieve the stag. Evgej waved the boy back. The gray bitch between Valam and Evgej had raised her tail and was pointing with her nose.

A doe raced into the clearing. Valam notched an arrow and waited. The doe was some distance to the left, and he had to turn sharply in the saddle to aim. He pulled the bowstring to his cheek, but a heartbeat before he released, two fawns followed the doe into the clearing.

Valam lowered his bow, as did the hunt master. Evgej's men were soon to follow. Between them they had several game hens and three rabbits—and something unexpected: a half-man, old and scrawny, dressed in rags. He was bound hand and foot and being dragged bodily by a burly hunter named Taggard. Taggard thrust the man at the feet of Valam's charger, and the horse whinnied but held steady.

The old man whirled around, turned his head to stare up at Valam. He was missing a hand and an ear. His eyes were wild but there was no fear.

Valam sat solemnly on his horse, his long black hair stirring in the wind. He had a detached cast to his green eyes, and he seemed suddenly more a prince and less a man. Seth, watching, thought Valam had taken off his face and donned the mask of Prince Valam Alder, Lord of South Province, heir to Great Kingdom's throne.

As Valam dismounted, saying "What have we here?" the old man kicked himself backward and away with his feet. Valam had never taken a squire, so Evgej's steward brought him his sword—an instrument of the king's justice. "Truth Bringer" the sword was called. It was wider across than a man's hand and taller than most men as well. The blade was the finest Reassae steel and sharp enough to part a man's head from his shoulders with but a single blow.

"Bandit or poacher?" Valam asked curtly.

The old man spat, continuing to kick his way backward. Valam stepped forward but made no move to strike a blow.

"Where did you find him?" Valam asked the hunters.

"Near the mammoth oak, no more than five hundred paces from here," one of the huntsmen replied.

"The Sentinel," Taggard added quickly, seeming to know the tree of which the others spoke.

Valam nodded knowingly.

The air was growing chill in the fading twilight and the breath of men and horses was heavy in the air. The hunters, their eyes on the growing shadows in the forest, seemed agitated. Evgej voiced quietly, but firmly, "My prince, I pray your justice will be swift. We should return to camp before night falls."

"Have the men return with the game; we are going to stay a little more."

"My prince, these woods are—"

Valam cut Evgej off, "You forget your place. This is South Province. Woods I know better than most men, even perhaps you, hunt master."

Evgej waved for the hunters to return to camp with their catch. Soon it was only the five of them: the hunt master, the elf, the steward, the prince, and the half-man.

Evgej dismounted, his expression dark. "There's a stump at the far end of the clearing that would serve, my lord prince."

Valam rested his boot on the half man's leg to stop his kicking. He leaned over, almost daring the other to spit again. "Shall it be to the stump then?" he asked.

The half-man stopped struggling, but did not speak.

"Your prince asked you a question," Evgej said, pulling the man to his feet. "Have you no tongue?"

"Oh, I've a tongue," the half man replied, "and I'm of the mind that what I say won't matter either way. So put me to the stump then and have done with it."

"I warned you the last time," Valam said.

"And so you did. Well then, so be it. I'm not afraid of death, only that the blow may stray or your steel may dull."

"Watch your words more carefully, I warn you."

The half-man grunted and huffed indignantly. "Like such alone would work."

Evgej looked quizzically at Valam. "You know this one, do you not?"

Valam cast a glance behind them, said quietly, "I do. Isn't that so Eldrick?" At the sound of his name the half-man squealed, though whether it was from displeasure or delight wasn't clear. "Tell him. Tell them both." He raised his sword. "Be quick about it. No mischief work; it is your last warning."

"And it is a fair one."

Valam slashed down with his sword. The other cringed, closed his eyes, waited, but the blow didn't strike him, instead it cut the bonds from his hands and feet. The half man opened one eye first and then the other, looking down, as if to make sure he still had all his parts. He raised his arms and danced in a circle, then dashed off into the forest before anyone could stop him.

"You let him go?"

"I did." Valam smiled, returning his great sword to his saddlebags then mounting. "Don't worry, he will not go far."

Evgej mounted and looked at the sky. The twilight was nearly gone. Soon the woods would be shrouded in darkness. His expression said he wanted to return to the camp, but he said nothing of it.

Seth, who had been silent throughout the encounter, mounted the gray courser. Valam led them deep into the forest of ash, elm and birch. Here and there they passed an oak, but they were few and far between. The shadows grew steadily as the canopy thickened and darkness settled in until only a pale light filtered down from the moon and distant stars above. Soon they were unable to go any farther on horseback and were forced to dismount, which was just as well, as limbs and thick boughs of trees were becoming treacherous to pass ahorse. Evgej's steward reluctantly stayed with the horses.

When they came to a small stream, Valam turned and began to follow it. Although the forest had become increasingly dense, on either side of the small stream a narrow path was clear and traversable.

The stream widened ahead, and beyond the widening lay a clearing. Valam pointed to something within the clearing.

The ground became wet as they progressed and their movements were slowed. The stream circled around a small island with a single ancient oak, which towered over it. Valam led them around to the far side, where there was a sort of bridge, and they crossed onto the tiny scrap of land.

"Can you feel it?" asked Valam.

They didn't have to ask what—they could feel it. The gentle swirling of the water, the soothing breeze, the serenity, it all fit.

"I discovered this place long ago; such summers I had then. I had been lost and alone and just when I thought I would never find my way out of the forest, I came upon this place and I didn't feel alone any—"

"—I wonder why," said a voice from up in the tree. The half-man hung upside down from a branch by his legs. "Could it be because you weren't alone any more? And you treating your benefactor so! You should be ashamed—"

"Watch your tongue, Eldrick, or I'll have it out."

"Yes, my lord," the half-man said sarcastically, "Should I kiss his royal lordship's—" Valam grabbed for the half-man's good arm at the same time Evgej did. Together they pulled him from the tree. He fell to the ground with a thump. "—I see I stand corrected."

"And so you do," Valam said. "What were you going to say?"

"Only to beg your forgiveness, my lord. Surely you've no gratitude for the help all those years ago."

"Change," Valam commanded.

"Must I?"

"You must."

The half-man glared and waved his arms. Where a moment ago he had worn rags for clothes, now finery few had ever seen graced his small frame; and in the place of wrinkles, shaggy beard, and long, unkempt hair was a fair, clean-shaven face, young by any standard. However, the eyes told of age beyond understanding by most. When the transformation was complete, the left ear and hand were missing no more.

"My forest brother," Seth whispered, grasping Eldrick's hand. "I thought your people long lost. We have but songs about your kind now in the Reach." He kneeled and was near tears.

Eldrick laughed and danced as he broke into soft song.

The brothers of the forest, they were a special breed.

In name, in hand, in deed they took the lead.

Oh Ash of spring forest, they were the first when all was new.

In the dawn of bloom and blossom they led us to the mew.

Yielding wood so strong and long to send the poison yew.

Oh Oak of summer forest, they were a special breed.

In the hot long days of sultry sun, they took the lead,

Giving shelter to our spirits and acorns for our feed.

Oh Pine of winter forest, they were tall and green and right.

In the dark hour of the cold, long night they were a delight.

Lending needle and cone to nestle us through the night.

ཀྵ In the Service of Dragons ཀྵ

Oh Elm of autumn forest, they kept on despite the blight.

In the twilight at the end of all, they showed their might

Arching branch and leaf to deliver us from our plight.

The brothers of the forest, they were a special breed.

In name, in hand, in deed they took the lead.

Valam stepped between Eldrick and Seth. "Enough! Trickster, charlatan. Don't play me or my friends for fools. Show your true self."

Eldrick frowned, the finery of his clothes fading to leaf green as he did so and branches replaced limbs. A glowing aura outlined his form and before Seth could step up and away, Eldrick stepped to the great oak. He disappeared within the tree, sending a glowing shimmer up the tree trunk to the thick boughs, then to branch and leaf. Soon the whole tree was aglow and the island as well all the way to the far banks of the stream.

Evgej touched the tree, his eyes full of wonder. Seth turned to Valam, exclaiming, "A tree spirit, that is just as well! In all my years, I have never had such privilege."

"Privilege? I'm not sure I would call it privilege. Eldrick gets what

Eldrick wants, isn't that so?"

The tree quivered and shook from branch and leaf, then a face appeared in the trunk. "It is so."

"It is truly a place of power," whispered Seth.

Evgej thought he was out of place here; he didn't belong. He was sharing an experience that he sensed should have been only between Seth and Valam.

"You would not be here if Eldrick did not want it so," thought Seth plainly to Evgej.

"You read thoughts too?"

"Don't worry Evgej. I think I can teach you a way to keep Seth out of your thoughts." Valam laughed.

"You can?"

"Yes, I think I can."

"And me?" asked the tree. Valam turned his back on the tree. "Not very nice; still such a reprehensible fellow."

"Let us go, Eldrick."

"My name grants you no power over me."

"What is it you want?"

Eldrick stepped out of the tree, became a half-man again, though without rags or finery, wrinkles, or semblance of youth. "You bring one of the wood folk to my forest and expect that I am not curious? It has been a thousand years since the fair folk walked beneath my boughs, and I would have the feeling of that joy again."

"And so you've had it. Now let us go."

"You are no prisoner here. You are free to go as you will."

"No tricks. We could not have turned away from this path had we wanted to. Is your curiosity so strong that you would bring an entire hunting party to your door?"

"It seems at times that I have but curiosity. What else is there for an old tree such as me?" Eldrick snorted. "Ho ho, I rhymed!"

"Let us go then."

"Not so fast. True, I wanted this meeting, but only as much as you. You wanted to test the fair one, knowing I wouldn't reveal myself to one who was untrue of heart, mind or spirit. I have, and the test is passed, so now you want to go on your way. I say again, not so fast." Eldrick whirled around to face Seth. "Ask?"

"It is said that the sentinel trees are in all the great forests. Oak in the summer forest, pine in the winter forest—"

"—ash in the spring forest, elm in the autumn forest. True, true, true, all true. All have sentinels and us, those who watch over the watchers."

"Yet there are no sentinel trees in the Reach?" It was a statement as much as a question.

"Ah, but there would be if you had taken us along on your journey to the new lands. We would be there all, oak and pine, ash and elm, which is why I aim to go with you."

Valam threw up his hands. "Not this day or any other, you trickster. What is it you really want?"

"So unkind, so untrue, so irrational, and I've to see my brother, and I will."

"Brother? You said there were no tree spirits in the Reach?"

"And that is where you aim to go ultimately, isn't it? You won't betray a friend for a father. You know it in your heart, don't you?" Eldrick didn't wait for an answer. He dashed into the tree, sending shimmering sparks up through the trunk, boughs and leaves of the great oak. He returned shortly afterward carrying a dusty gray cloak, a staff crowned with a carved bear's head, and a worn leather bag with a broken handle. "Ready, shall we be going then?"

Evgej laughed. Valam scowled. Seth offered to help Eldrick carry his gear, but the half-man waved him off. The four didn't say much else after that. They remained awhile longer, though, and drank in the peace of the Sentinel. As they left, Evgej didn't feel such an outsider anymore; he had shared something with Seth and Valam that no others had, and he marveled at their wondrous new companion.

Eldrick led the way back to the waiting horses. They proceeded in pairs: Eldrick and Valam, Seth and Evgej. Eldrick and Seth, who could see in the dark, kept the other two from hitting branches and stumbling over obstacles at their feet. Soon the steward was calling out, "Who goes there? Show yourselves?" in a fearful voice.

"Only I, Derworth," Evgej called back, "and the prince and his fellows."

Derworth never asked who the prince's fellows were though he could scarcely see in the dark. When they returned to camp, it was evident they had been missed. Father Jacob was furious, but his anger lessened when those who had been sent out to search for the prince returned without incident.

The group broke camp as the first light of day broke the horizon, hoping to reach Quashan' by late afternoon of the second day. No one inquired about the strange new companion who rode behind Seth on a white palfrey. No one offered any information either.

Mysteriously, though, no one saw the stranger again after the group stopped for their midday meal. As they rode, Valam looked to the four corners of the world in search of Eldrick but saw no one and nothing out of the ordinary. He knew with certainty he would meet Eldrick again, and in all probability in the most unlikely of circumstances.

4

Amir emerged from shadow and bent down to pick up the orb, shouting, "He lives! He has returned! I have seen it with my own eyes!"

Noman thought to say, "Are you sure? Can you be certain?" but the look in Amir's eyes answered the questions for him. He asked instead, "Do they know?"

"He drank in the mortal wounds of the Gray Lord as if they were nothing. There can be no doubt. He has returned. It has come to pass."

"There is no warrant in foretelling only truth," Noman said as he cast the sticks upon the oaken table, promising himself that it would be his final look at the paths of destiny until what needed to be done was done. Sometimes he thought they were all fools upon the board, he the greatest fool of them all; and like a fool he moved forward only to find that he must move backward.

ଛୀଔ In the Service of Dragons ଛୀଔ

A vast weight was upon his shoulders as if he were the last pillar upon which all of Over-Earth rested. He was the Keeper of the Sky but what remained of the Sky? The Titans, eagle lords and dragons of the realm were all but gone. He was spent, the husk of what he had once been, and for a moment, all but fleeting, he thought of her. She was reborn as well, as was her fate. Unlike him, she would have no memories of days past until the very last when it ended in pain as it always did.

"Why Adrynne?" he asked in a whisper. In his mind, he followed the War of Tears. He saw Stranth victorious in Pakchek. The forced march along the Path. The conquering of Oshio. The long drive along the Wish to Papiosse. A further victory turned to bitter dust along with the Defeat. "You would have been Queen over all."

Amir touched Noman's shoulder. "You speak in whispers."

Noman tried to look up from the morass of black, gray and white spread out on the table before him; but before he could turn away, it became a spinning vortex that sought to suck him into the nothingness of shadow. He braced himself and fought frantically to push away as past days spun before eyes he could not close.

"You are a Ruler of Right and Knight of the Blood. One of the Nine Sons of the Blood," cried out the Father of Blood in the spinning vortex. "I am the Tenth Son of the Blood; you will do as commanded."

"Never!" Noman shouted as he cast the sticks aside, sweeping them from the table. Blood trickled from the corners of his eyes as he turned around, wildly flailing his arms.

Amir steadied Noman. There was no alarm in his eyes, only concern, as he said, "The days of the Bloodrule are long gone. You are safe in the City of the Sky."

"It was as it had to be; it could not have been otherwise. I could not have done otherwise."

"There is no blame here, only truth," Amir said, using Noman's own words from past lessons.

"You must go," Noman said suddenly, pulling away from Amir. "Show them the path, but do not make the way an easy one."

When Amir disappeared from sight, Noman hastily retrieved the Destiny Sticks from the floor and rushed to his chambers. He found the staff where he had left it, nodded satisfaction, then put on his robe of colors. He tapped the staff against the floor, gripped the ancient carving at its crown and spoke the words of power, "Starod sil, otkry ot zemlya i pozhar, veter i vod!"

He disappeared into shadow and reappeared outside a door in a long hallway. One side of the hallway was open, and looked out to an expansive garden. In the center of the garden was a fountain whose hot waters gushed from the earth and bubbled with sulphur. Far across the palace, a bell began to toll or at least it sounded like the tolling of a bell to Noman, as he turned about on his heel and went to the door.

✳ ✳ ✳

Not a word passed between them. They simply stared in awe at the boy who lay curled up on the now dry ground next to the warmth of a low, softly crackling fire. The time the Watcher had spent the whole of his life in search of was near and it seemed to him he had briefly become the controlled when he had always thought of himself as the controller.

Privately, he berated himself for not attuning to his surroundings better; for now that he searched out the source of the evil, he found it was many days old and surprisingly strong—a doorway between the world of light and the world of darkness was open. Yet there were stronger forces at work than the unseen hands of evil, forces that beckoned and directed, forces that fed thoughts into their minds at levels that even the great shaman or the ancient lord could not fathom.

As he stared into the darkness of the night, Ayrian gave thanks to Father Wind for the life that flowed through him. He embraced remembrance as well, for the touch of the wanderer had brought with it a lucid dream of the past. In the dream, the Eagle Clans reigned freely in the mountain valleys of the northern ranges once again. The Gray Clan held the longest range from two snowcaps east of Solstice Mountain to the shallow foothills midway into the westlands. He recalled the presence of men—in the dream his feathers were not so full of silver as they were now. The men came seeking passage to the North and it was the White Clan that showed them the way. As men moved north, they brought with them their ways and the ways of the eagle clans—and indeed the eagle lords themselves—slowly died.

Memory faded. The night ended and the time of worship came. Ayrian began his morning prayers, his songs of praise to the creator and the preserver. It was this monotonic worship that roused Vilmos and awoke Xith to the sunrise. An energy loomed behind Vilmos' eyes, but beyond that, he seemed himself again.

Breakfast—oats and hardtack black bread—was prepared over the expiring coals of the fire. The first words to pass Vilmos' lips were "I hate dried oats" to which Xith replied with a chuckle, "I know, I know."

Finishing his morning worship, Ayrian joined Vilmos and Xith beside the fire as they finished breakfast. He ate lightly, his strange eyes never straying far from the gray and white facade of the distant mountains. Hills lay at the foot of those mountains, long and rolling, and before them stretched many miles of the rough country of the Borderlands, yet he saw only the mountains, distant and proud. Momentarily he thought of the sacred city of the clouds, a place that even in the zenith of his people had been taboo, banned for all time.

"We have a fair distance to travel, old friend, do we not?" Ayrian asked. Long ago, he had heard rumors from the White Clan, whose domain ran east from the territories of the Gray and included Solstice Mountain, that there were those among the Eagle Lords who had made the lofty ascent to the cold, dark summit that lay hidden from sight. It was said that a force as old as the earth itself walked the forbidden halls of the timeless city, a being that was kin to Great Father and Mother Earth, yet not of their direct lineage; and that this single being was the watch mark of all the maladies of the world who could not only see the paths of past, present and future but could also levy control to them, which was a skill the Father and Mother denied themselves.

"Yes, a long way to go, old friend. Will you lead the way from the skies?"

"Where are we going?" Vilmos asked.

Xith looked to Ayrian and smiled. "You will know it when we come to it, I am sure. Come, the fire has faded and that is as good a sign as any that we should make our departure."

✳ ✳ ✳

Noman knocked once, then opened the door. A large oak desk piled high with books and scrolls filled most of the room. Two chairs, arranged in front of the desk, were occupied as was the chair behind the desk. "I would speak with you alone, Keeper Martin," Noman said, dismissing the other two without a second thought.

Keeper Martin stood. "Sit, if you like," he said, offering no deference. He stretched out a hand, indicating one of the chairs off to the side of the desk. He nodded to Keeper Q'yer and Keeper Parren as they left the room and closed the door behind them. "Are you hungry? Shall I order food?"

"Gladly, some other time."

"As you say."

Noman looked to the door. "Can we—"

Keeper Martin lifted a hand, pointed to something he had written on a piece of parchment. "Will you take some wine then?'

"I would be pleased, thank you."

Keeper Martin took two glasses and a bottle of wine from the cabinet behind him. He poured one glass, passed the bottle and the other glass to Noman. Noman poured as Martin went to the other side of the room and brought a book from the far shelf.

"Ah, the Book of the Peoples, that is the very one. Thank you." A touch of his finger painted a reply, then he slipped the piece of parchment to Martin as he took the book.

Martin drank his wine, tucking the parchment into his pocket as he did so. "Would you care to take a walk in the gardens?"

"Perhaps another time."

"Another time then."

Noman finished his wine and left. He walked the length of the long hall, waiting until he was fully out of view from prying eyes before tapping his staff to the ground. As he started to say the words of power, a hand gripped his and pulled him through a hidden doorway.

"Master Keeper, you cannot leave, I need to know more," Keeper Martin whispered.

"It is what I know, all I know for now."

"It can't be so, it can't be."

"Martin Braddabaggon, you will know when it is time. You walk in

Imsa's footsteps. He knew and you will know as well. His blood is in you. You are a Braddabaggon and Head of the High Council of Keepers. You must go to Quashan' at once."

"I cannot hope to achieve what my grand—"

"—Alliances are made and broken; it is the way of things. If need be, seek out the Hand on the Wall, but only at your dire peril."

"The Hand on the Wall," Martin replied.

"Do not lose faith, Martin. It is as it is meant to be," and so saying, Noman struck his staff against the ground and spoke the words "Starod sil, otkry ot zemlya i pozhar, veter i vod!" There was urgency in his actions and tone—he truly needed to gather strength from the ancient elements of earth, fire, water and air as the words of power entreated.

Oh Adrynne, why? he asked himself as he disappeared into shadow.

5

The rough lands in the border country drained their strength as they trudged day in and out through jagged, rock-strewn land that grew steadily rougher and wilder the farther the three traveled. It seemed that they had nothing to look forward to save the mountains marking the boundary to the northern lands inching closer and closer, seeming increasingly insurmountable. During the day the land was hot and parched; at night it was windswept and frigid. The few scrub trees that dotted the earth provided only meager fires, which only tempted them with warmth.

The sound of animals scurrying about in the night was the most prevalent thing on Vilmos' mind. Carrion beasts occupied the skies of the day, ever vigilant in their search for the end of life and the beginning of their next meal. It was these creatures that Vilmos imagined when the night came, edging closer and closer, standing over him when the frequent clouds brought shadows across his eyes.

Thinking of carrion beasts helped him forget the memory of fighting his mirror-self. Each move he made, his other self made the same move, and the struggle was relentless. Where his two selves touched they merged, blending one into the other, sometimes twisting and bending one around the other, or warping and fusing so the lines between them blurred. Eventually, always, the lower torsos became one and it was only the upper bodies that were two.

As they locked arms and pressed against each other, each trying to gain control over the other, the two chests fused, bringing a terrible pain. The white-hot pain moved from his navel to his neck. Afterward it was only the two heads facing each other, looking out from one body, that remained separate one from the other. Relief came for an instant when his two selves faced each other for a final time. As the two heads merged, they echoed one within the other until finally both selves acquiesced and struggled no more. A flood of memories followed, both ancient and new, and then, like now, Vilmos was left with what little he could grasp of it all.

Xith walked beside Vilmos and called out, "You have that look again."

"I know I must," Vilmos said truly, "But how can a boy be a man and a man be a boy? And if—"

"It will all balance out. Much of what seems new will also seem familiar."

"Eh ho to we, to no wa," Ayrian said on wing from above them, "You are reborn, as are all things."

"A to no ma, as are you," Vilmos replied reflexively.

Ayrian called out in what sounded to Vilmos like laughter as he thrust out with his great wings and raced ahead.

The day passed, as did many others. Vilmos started to think that the Borderlands were aptly named. The land itself was unpredictable; at its southerly skirt lay jagged hills that seemed to flow up the western perimeter and meld into the rolling hills that formed its northerly bounds, yet in between were arid lands that went from flat, endless wastes strewn with stunted growths to odd, patchy lands that seemed to be heaved up from the darkest bowels of the earth itself. It was the latter that the trio traversed presently. Vilmos cringed and cursed as they passed yet another abysmal fissure around which were allayed great juttings of rock that looked as if the earth had spat them out.

There was obvious tension in the air; Vilmos sensed it, though no one spoke of it. He recalled now the previous night's discussion, one that the shaman and the eagle lord had not meant for him to hear. The two spoke briefly and in hushed tones of the Hunter Clan. Apparently, Ayrian had spotted a small group of them the day before; yet as far as he could tell they were not being pursued by the Hunter Clan.

The following day brought Vilmos, Xith and Ayrian to the first of the foothills that gradually spread out toward the mountains, and only then did the perceived tension diminish. At first Vilmos greeted the arrival of the hills as a blessing, but this feeling of good fortune was rapidly replaced by indifference as nightfall came and found them still trekking through the hill country. The whole next day became a slow battle against a rolling land that seemed to have the upper hand. Vilmos' feet were sore and blistered by the time they finally reached the first path that led up into the mountains.

"Solstice Mountain," Ayrian called out from above before winging his way up the mountain. The sense of jubilation faded when Xith told Vilmos that the trail before them only led up into the narrow gap that spread between the great range, and that they would travel only partially along its course before veering off into the heart of the mountain; yet as he touched the first of his footfalls to the stone of the mountain and with each step he took, it did seem that a veil was slowly being lifted from before his eyes.

For Xith and Vilmos, the first few hundred yards of the climb were the easiest, yet from there the climb became a steadily increasing challenge. The ancient path up into the gap was worn by rains and washouts, and in several places it was as if a perpendicular rock wall had been thrown up in front of them. Ayrian used his great wings to scout the trail ahead and became instrumental in their successful progress many times.

They climbed sharply up through the mountains long after the earth was swept with darkness; they climbed, finally stopping only when the path's end lay before them. The moderate starlight that had guided them still gave them light as they set up a meager camp. Their level of anxiety was high as they thought of the events that tomorrow would bring. For that reason, sleep was elusive this night although it should have come easily after an exhausting day.

A new day came with heavy cloud cover, which gradually thinned out as the day passed and hopes and expectations soared; somewhere aloft lay the mystical city of the clouds, and all they needed to do was attain the summit and the city would be theirs. The sun blazed high across the mountaintops and still they climbed though soon they would reach the fog layer shrouding the uppermost reaches of the peak, and from there they did not know how far the climb would be. They turned from the trail near the gap, following another smaller path that led upward into the foggy shroud. This path was like the one that continued through the gap and then split, becoming two other trails that slowly wound their way down through the mountains eventually taking its travelers into the northlands. It was a remnant of what had once been a large, well-worn trail. Now it consisted only of large clear patches followed by sparse stretches of ice that wound their way up the mountain at an angle that curved up and across its face. And slowly they progressed along it. Ayrian, with his great wings, helped the two make it through the many areas that would have been insurmountable otherwise. However, as they entered the foggy shroud that loomed over the whole of the lofty precipice like a great white blanket, the advantage disappeared, and a new arena where no one knew what was ahead lay before them.

The ground beneath their feet began to gather larger amounts of water, feeling cool at first to tired, burning muscles, turning hard as it slowly turned to a frozen sheet. The air thinned in tune with the freezing of the land, and pauses for reprieve became increasingly necessary. When they stopped, which was with growing frequency, Xith and Vilmos brought the cowls of their cloaks close against their faces and gathered numb hands into their lower folds, the cold only then seeming to bite into their skin. Ayrian was the sole member of the group that had little difficulty coping in the extremes; the cold had little effect on him, and to him the air seemed fresher at higher altitudes.

Snow far more abundant than the ice replaced it; and just when the path was completely lost to their eyes, they were surprised to find that they were near the peak. Temporarily, the heavy weariness faded away; and they charged up the sharp rise toward the summit. Hearts and minds raced, for it seemed that the journey was finally at an end. Vilmos slipped and fell twice in the steep, quick ascent, nearly slamming his knee into a sharp rock one time, and the other nearly falling face first onto a similar dark, forbidding stone. The exhausted trio stood still and silent when at last they attained the mighty crown of Solstice Mountain—a jagged pinnacle of ice, snow, and rock gathered in a foggy shroud—unsure where to proceed, for here their combined knowledge ended. Xith had never been here before although he knew that this was where they must go, nor had Ayrian; and Vilmos was confused. Vilmos had said nothing during the latter stage of the climb; his mind had been filled with shadows and lurking specters from the distant past. He knew this place from somewhere yet couldn't quite grasp how.

The boy looked from the Watcher to Ayrian, back and forth, back and forth. He began to trudge through the snow toward the steeply descending cliff ahead of him, drawn by a seemingly nonchalant hand. The other two eventually followed. A barely visible circular platform void of snow and ice hung at the very fringe of the dark, gray cliff. The platform was plain and unremarkable except for three small sets of stairs in the middle that led upward and outward, ending in open air.

Xith began to climb the stairs but Vilmos stopped him with a wavering hand.

"That is the fools' gambit," came the peculiarly familiar voice from within him, "we must wait."

While the boy crouched to his haunches and settled in to wait, Xith tossed a nervous glare at Ayrian and then they did likewise. The sky about them slowly turned deeper shades of gray and then became utter black. Night settled in about them; and as it brought about a shift in temperatures, the haze began to thin and a clear, moonless night with no clouds to mar it tardily appeared. Below the platform's perch a thick blanket of white glistened, looking as if one could walk out across it to the neighboring mountain peaks. Above, as moonrise came, the stars twinkled and shone; it was a full autumn moon that sadly looked down on the unlikely trio. From high above, two others carefully watched; unseen, they studied each in turn. The presence did not astound or confound them; there was no quandary in the arrival. The two were known to them, yet it was the third who distressed them.

"The time to act is now!" intoned the older of the two.

"Yes, the waiting is at last over."

"Go, do what you must."

"Yes, master," said Amir as he disappeared, to reappear on the platform below in the midst of those gathered there.

The strange and powerful-looking newcomer slowly withdrew his sword from its embellished scabbard; the double-edged blade was as long as Vilmos was tall and finely honed. It cheerfully reflected the light of the sad autumn moon. Ayrian was about to react when a gentle hand steadied his arm. The birdman cocked his head in his odd fashion, turning to regard the hand on his shoulder; there was a distant, knowing stare in the eyes of its owner. Ayrian and Xith studied the great one before them; the description they vaguely recalled from ancient lore although they had never personally met the son of the titan king.

"We seek entrance into your city. The time is now, *Sentinel*." issued the voice from Vilmos.

As before, Amir knew the voice but not the face of the third; the voice he recalled from a distant time, a time of strife and turmoil. Having eyes that could see into this realm and beyond into shadow heightened his other senses. A sense of trust flowed through his mind concerning the first two; still, the other worried him. He perceived only an empty space in his mind where feelings for the third should have been, yet it was the latter that had known the ancient name of invocation. He had somehow expected this strange boy, who was not a boy, to know the commanding word; so his suspicion did not dwindle, it only grew. He sheathed his weapon, and in the next instant all four stood in the audience room of the Cloud City. The audience chamber was a long hall with a high vaulted ceiling shaped in the symmetry of three waning moons and in each of the three circular corners of the chamber stood a mural. Together they told a story of the world's past, and they seemed to change with the passing of time. Noman let them drink in the ambiance before he blighted the air with spoken words. He saw the tension in Amir, yet said nothing to allow him to relax; the time was here at last, and now the sentinel must forever be at the ready.

"Welcome to the City of the Sky, Shaman of the Great Northern Reaches, Lord of the Gray Eagle Clan, and lastly, the wanderer who has come home. I am Noman, guardian of the lost children of the Father, master of the City of the Sky, and my companion is Amir, a child of the Blood Wars. Your arrival here marks the beginning—"

"—of the end." interrupted Vilmos. "Very dark times are ahead; the world will fall to utter chaos. There can be no stopping it, for even if you tried you could not, for it must be. Soon the world will be divided as chaos begins. The armies grow, the beasts emerge from their burrows, the dark forces reborn will incite the kingdoms to war and to civil strife, and the kingdoms will fall one by one. All civilization will be laid to ruin.

"Out of the chaos will come an ending of the old and a beginning of the new. For now we must seek out the child of the coming, then the gathering will truly begin. Are you surprised? I too know the words of the prophecy. Prophecies come and go, old man."

Noman stared down at the boy in wonder.

"True, true, all true, time will be the judge. Where is the other? Did you not find her?" The latter was directed at Xith.

"Yes, I found her, though I fear we must hurry. They have already found us once."

The guardian's face turned suddenly grim and he spoke again but his words were lost in the echoes of the tremendous hall, but to Xith it sounded as if he had said, "Yes, yes, and many, many more along the way."

6

Feelings of relief spread rapidly throughout the group when the city came into view. The sun, surprisingly, had only begun its descent towards the horizon. The city honor guard hastened them to the gates, where Chancellor Van'te welcomed them to the city. A cheer arose from the men as Valam announced that they were to be assigned quarters and then released to wander the city as they would. He also promised to ensure that the city's taverns flowed with ale until the last man passed out.

A small contingent of honor guard, those who had accompanied Valam to Imtal, waited patiently for their instructions. They were still mounted and seated quietly. Valam was just about to mount when a soft voice reached him.

"Lord Valam, may I have a word with you?" quietly, respectfully intoned one of the mounted guard.

"Why, of course," said Valam. Chancellor Van'te was quick to whisper a name in the prince's ear. Valam smoothly appended, "Bowman Ylsa."

"I don't know if you have noticed, my lord, but I am not a man," the woman spoke kindly, not harshly as she dismounted. Ylsa unbundled her hair and let it flow long. "I prefer the title of Archer if you do not mind."

"I— I— I—" stuttered Valam.

The chancellor whispered in his ear again, "Strong spirited, isn't she?" The chancellor scrutinized Ylsa closely now, smiling.

"Yes, yes indeed," said Valam louder than he wished in reply to Van'te's statement.

"Good," said Ylsa smiling, "have a pleasant evening, my lord, prince."

Ylsa turned and walked away, leading her mount behind her.

"She is a Bowman First Rank," intoned the chancellor happily, "Do you wish to know more? I will gladly inquire for you."

"No, Chancellor Van'te. I do not wish to know more. Thank you."

The chancellor smiled a devilish smile, knowing the frustrated tone of his lord prince. He would tell Isador of this one; perhaps she could spark an interest as a concubine, forcing him to a wife of standing.

The palace proper was a short distance away; and once within its guarded walls, Valam felt he had truly come home. Quashan' palace wasn't as grand as Imtal's. It didn't have grand gardens stretching through numerous courtyards or sanctioned council halls. It was a simple four-towered castle with a meager courtyard, a fair-sized armory, and a modest stable.

The gatehouse held, but a single shielding portcullis and inner rampart had only recently been rebuilt. The palace proper was a separate building, two stories in height, that sat squarely in the center of the rear bastion. Still, Valam admired its simple beauty as he waited for a stable boy to retrieve his mount, telling the boy to make certain that he had rubbed the horse down fully before he turned in for the night.

Chancellor Van'te quickly had hot baths drawn for Valam, Seth, and Father Jacob, insisting that they bathe and rest before they held any type of council. Introductions, although extremely cordial, were very brief.

When they were suitably rested, the chancellor returned. He ushered them downstairs, telling them someone was waiting for them, an old acquaintance. At the same time, Seth and Valam thought, Adrina, and asked where she was. Van'te assured them it was not any one Valam knew, rather an old friend of Seth's, which perplexed both Seth and Valam.

"Why all the mystery?" asked Valam.

"Would you spoil an old man's fun?" asked Chancellor Van'te.

"And mine!" responded another.

Seth recognized the voice, or at least he thought he recognized the voice, though it could not be.

"Yes, your hearing is fine, Brother Seth, first of the order of the Red, protector of the Queen-Mother."

"But *how?*" asked Seth in disbelief.

"I am quite tough myself," said the man behind the voice, as he stepped out of the shadows to embrace Seth.

Valam was totally lost; he had never seen this stranger before, nor had Van'te mentioned him in any of the messages to his father.

"The Great-Father must still have plans for me."

Valam fixed Chancellor Van'te with angry eyes.

"Why didn't you tell me?"

"He only arrived here early last week. Your group had already departed when the message reached Imtal Palace."

"How is it that we missed your messenger on the road?" asked Valam skeptically.

"Honest, my lord, he went via Veter and then on to Imtal."

"It is truly great to see you again!" exclaimed Seth.

Valam was still confused. The man appeared to be of the same stature as Seth, the skin color was the same, the hair, the eyes, yet he seemed to lack something. Valam couldn't quite place what it was. When formal introductions were finally made, Valam and Van'te excused themselves to allow the two friends to catch up on the past.

Seth and Cagan talked long into the night. Seth first explained his experiences in Imtal and then Cagan told how he had come to meet Chancellor Van'te. He spoke of the blind man who had found and befriended him and mended his broken leg and treated his wounds. The saltwater had fouled the wounds and nearly rotted the leg. Poison was festering and spreading through his body. He had almost lost his leg and his life, but the old gentleman had been able to save them both.

Afterwards, there was nothing more the two could say, so they retired to their beds, seeking to catch as much sleep as possible before the sun rose high in the heavens. As Seth lay in bed, he thought back to the last time he had seen Cagan. It had been just before the ship went down. His mind jumped to the letter Cagan had given him in those few frantic moments in which the Queen-Mother spoke of what he must do and why. No matter the cost, the two must survive. Seth had learned of his fate that day and it had carried him through experiences he would not have endured otherwise.

His mind exploded as the rationalization hit him; he now understood the Queen-Mother's cryptic message. The Father had already seen to their needs. He had been blind in his thinking about Galan; if his mind had been open, he would have known that the Father would not have let them fail. He had denied fate and tempted destiny. Galan should have been allowed to pass; it was her time and now she was gone forever. She did not even rest in the house of the Father.

Images flashed through his mind. Seth could not deny the feelings of guilt. His thoughts were scattered to and fro. He tried to close his tired eyes and find solace in sleep, yet the face came to him and would not allow him to do so. As he lay staring at the ceiling, another face danced within his thoughts and even in sleep the two faces found him.

Valam had not been idle the previous night; he and the good chancellor stayed up well into the early morning hours discussing plans for the camp to be set up near the coast, the progress of arms production, the acquisition of supplies, and many other things. The rumors of continued unrest in the Minors wandered into their conversation from time to time though the chancellor seemed to think the rumors were idle chatter. Valam was inclined to believe him. They had many contacts in each of the kingdoms and if something were really taking place, they would know.

Over the course of the next several days, the base camp was constructed, and training and recruitment began. Once the camp was set up and supplies and arms were distributed, Valam's fears concerning the other kingdoms disappeared. Runners were sent to all areas of the kingdom, including the major cities of the north and east. Valam intentionally sent two sets of runners to Imtal and within days those that had been gathering around the city and those that were filling its guest houses, inns and streets, quickly raced southward.

Word of mouth spread fastest through the countryside and after a time Valam sent out no more runners. He allowed rumors and excitement to do the work that it would have taken his runners a fortnight to do. The camp, which was already of generous proportions, housing a massive contingent that represented nearly a third of the Imtal garrison, a select stock from the garrison outposts along the route from Imtal to Quashan', and a healthy number of mercenaries from the Free Cities, nearly doubled in seven days, yet it wasn't only soldiers and mercenaries that joined the encampment. Peddlers, merchants, and hustlers of all sorts descended upon the camp. Valam found that he had his hands full just controlling the crowds.

Perimeter patrols were set up around the camp along with a continuous watch. Controlled checkpoints were erected at the four ordinal points of the compass. Mounted patrols rode constantly, surveying the area the soldiers now referred to as Peddler Town, a place where nearly everything that could be bought or sold in the Free Cities was readily available. A fence had to be erected around the training grounds to hold back the spectators and this seemed to be the thing that set Valam on fire.

A decree went forth written in Chancellor Van'te's own hand. Those that defied the patrols would no longer be set free or levied with a simple fine. A mandatory sentence of servitude was called for—service in the army of Great Kingdom until the transgressors had fulfilled their obligation to the state. Suddenly, and without much surprise, Peddler Town quieted, the patrols no longer had difficulties twenty-four hours a day, and the training grounds were vacated during practice hours. A disturbance happened now and then, but only a few times a day, which Valam counted as a divine gift.

7

Beyond the grand audience chamber lay a central athenaeum, gathering halls, dining halls, kitchens, rows of bed chambers, open air courtyards and many, many other chambers of various kinds, yet it was the bathing pool that drew in the tired, grimy travelers. Boyish airs returned to Vilmos as he playfully swam around the large oval pool, and Ayrian and Xith watched with surprised interest.

Hidden things stirred within the boy; and they awaited the time of their further arousal, which could still be years away. This first day in the mystical city passed as a blur before their eyes, and none would be able to recall it in the days or weeks that followed.

Lacking a discernible day or night, the Cloud City truly seemed outside of time; and for the most part throughout the many days that followed their arrival, Vilmos was left to his own whims while the shaman and the lord spent most of their time in heated debates with the master of the

Cloud City, Noman. On the other hand, the gentle warrior, Amir, was free-roaming; and, as he wasn't the sort to enter into the discussions, he spent most of the time with Vilmos.

Vilmos was intrigued by the goliath and his play with the sword, watching with earnest interest during the periods when Amir trained, imagining the shadow dancing around the nimble warrior. Often he would laugh, shriek, and even applaud. Xith, however, did not spend all of his time with Noman; he also made time to continue the boy's training and education.

Vilmos was more curious than ever about magic and its origins. He came to realize, in his experience in the Cloud City, that it was not evil as he had been led to believe in the past. Xith also did this to see how far the black priests had corrupted the boy's thinking and if this twisting could be undone.

Outside, beyond the sanctified walls, a fortnight had passed though within the City a mere seven days had taken place. The moon was again full and the night sky was cloudless and full of brightly shining stars although those within did not know this. Amir had paced nervously throughout most of the day; and now as the others ate the evening meal in the grand dining hall beneath the wide sphere of the central dome, he again roamed in front of a nearby window.

A decision had been made the previous day to leave the city of the sky, and this would be the group's last meal within the great, protective walls. Among the many thoughts that disturbed the agile warrior's thoughts, this was the one that played most heavily, for he did not wish to venture beyond the sanctuary the great walls afforded.

"What is wrong with him?" asked Vilmos, indicating the solemn figure of Amir.

"He is troubled, that is all; it will pass," replied Noman.

"Eat, Vilmos, eat. We have much work to do, many studies to review," urged Xith. "Did you forget your promise?"

Vilmos frowned and returned his attention to his plate.

"What do you think will come of it?" asked Amir, making the long trek back to the table with slow precision as he spoke, "I mean, what will it all bring, for I can sense nothing but futility. It seems that the past will repeat itself and I cannot swallow the weight of it. I will not let it replay master, I can not."

Noman smiled, a generous smile that the newcomers were beginning to equate with the guardian's twisted sense of the just and the unjust.

"No single person can hold the weight of such a burden in the palm of his hand and be expected not to buckle beneath it, yet—" the savvy guardian paused purposefully, gripping clenched hands into tight fists, and all eyes turned to meet his unwavering gaze, especially those of the perceptive boy, "— yet, if we all perform a simple feat, such as twisting our hands at the wrist and turning them palms up and fingers spread wide—just like this—"

Noman demonstrated.

"We can reach out—go ahead, reach out—and intertwining our fingers, one within the other, we can lock them together and thus we can all, leaving no single one without his share, bear the weight of the burden. None of the united will buckle under the shared weight."

As Noman finished, his voice trailing off and fading into echoes that wandered the hall, the air seemed alive with energy; and by way of the link of hands that circled around the table, it surged through the collective group. Upon later reflection, that one fleeting moment would be the shaman's fondest recollection of the time spent within the mystical city, and the spell of bonding woven in that same instant would cling to the hearts of the other listeners with an equal sense of affection for a long, long time. Yet even the influence of such potency could not protect the ill-fated group from what happened next.

"Master, *they* come!" yelled Amir as he drew his sword and leaped from the platform where the group was seated to the large open floor and then back again in a single, fluid seesaw motion.

As if in answer, the walls and ceiling of the chamber imploded, sending debris cascading in all directions. Noman quickly managed a defensive barrier, a great magical shield, and most of the debris fell harmlessly away. Open to the night sky, the chamber was a gaping hole of emptiness that gazed up into the dark night sky, and with the darkness came a bitter cold that swept through the chamber. A figure stood apart from the others, away from Noman's protective shield, gathered in a shimmering shroud of light that shifted and fluttered as if it were a part of the very air that the figure breathed. A few moments passed, no more than a collection of sporadic heartbeats for the onlookers, but it became clear who the figure was; and it wasn't shock or dismay that traversed the many deep-set lines stemming from forehead to chin but fear, simple fear.

Beneath the protection of Noman's magical dome, the four watched and waited. Amir had his sword held at the ready, Xith yanked in the energies from around him, shaping the wild magic to his own whims, and Ayrian flexed his wings, preparing to act on his notion to launch into the sky. None of the four could have predicted what was to occur next, not even the wisest among them who had seen the many paths the future held and followed the many turnings. A new branching had broken from the main path moments before. The dark shapes stirred in the night sky, shifting amongst the stars, moving closer until they blocked out the light from above as they clustered around the fallen roof. The whole chamber became enshrouded in shadows with the exception of the glowing figure and the translucent barrier Noman maintained. A new path was being shaped.

"Here me, O Dark Ones! You shall return to your masters either in defeat or victory this day, but let it be known that I, Dalphan, the Wanderer-Reborn, *He* that in his madness was once Rapir the Black, dissolve the dark pact with his brothers. My spirit will not rest until you return to darkness and then, only then, at the last shall I return the watcher to the gate—for all time."

The warning not heeded, the servants of the darkness continued to descend from the sky. They were not ready to return to the void, and no single being would make them return without the cost of their dark lives. In their eyes, the four mortals before them and one who had once been a favored son were no match for a dark army that cried out at its own rebirth. Mrak, the wraith king, came to the fore, his shadow-like face seeming oddly saddened—if sadness was an emotion such creatures were capable of feeling. Dalphan motioned for the others not to attack as Mrak approached.

"Why, master?" came the raspy, whispered voice, "The plan was flawless."

"I am not what I once was. I have changed. I remember the past, and I cannot let it be replayed. Leave now, my friend, and I will spare your life. There are places in this world as yet untouched and they could be yours."

"I cannot," said Mrak sadly, "The world of darkness and the world of light feed off of one another. Where there are souls I must go. You know this—and yet you entreat with such folly."

"You must!" the other disagreed.

"I am sorry," said Mrak, his features growing cold and rigid as he spoke. Mrak pointed a long sinewy finger down at Xith and Ayrian, saying in the same raspy, half-whispered voice, "I should have claimed your spirits when I had the chance!"

Mrak ascended back into the ranks of the servants; and poised there behind his kind, he looked down with true sadness at his old master. He was sure he would not endure this night, yet he was also sure his master would not either.

In waves, the creatures of darkness and dread descended like a grave blanket to the floor of the dome, with the more powerful wraiths lingering at the rear. Although his thoughts fixed on a distant figure, Amir rushed to cut off the first such group, hags of the night, creatures with corporeal bodies, pawns of darkness. He was lightning with his sword, lashing out repeatedly, ripping clean the rotting flesh from the beasts; and each time he struck, one of the creatures fell. He surged forward through their ranks, cutting a straight path towards the one who waited for him. The trapped soul within the hag was different from those of the wraiths or the other dark beings gathered before them, for it was not entirely twisted and bent towards evil ends. With the corporeal form the soul was offered a place of refuge from torment and within this form there remained bits and pieces of what had once been individual discernment, and this caused them to both fear and greet the return to darkness with an unsettling expectancy that chilled Amir.

Dazzling clashes of cobalt and vermilion light filled the chamber and reflected from the remains of the once proud walls as energies struck opposing magic shields. Only through deep concentration that required all his will did Noman maintain the shield against the combined onslaught. The masses, hags of the night, demons lesser and greater, specters and wraiths, continued to pour in through the broken dome crowding hungrily into the large space overhead and onto the floor of the dome. Behind them all, even behind the wraith king, far, far out, looking on, floated the nameless beast, the marshaler of darkness, mortal adversary of Amir the White, right hand of Sathar the Dark.

As each new wave of assault opened, it created another hole in the shield Noman continually replaced and refortified. Noman cringed and shrank back with each new bombardment. The cloistered demons were the heavy-handed dealers of magic for the dark forces; their shelter was largely the masses of their brethren crowded before them. A few among them did maintain protective barriers, but these were the lesser among them. They struck out with the forces of fire and negation, energies only they could interweave. From under the protective umbrella of Noman's shield, Xith struck back with his own offensive, causing even greater clashes of magic to rock the chamber. He understood the life force the demons held and the powers they tapped, and he used this to his fullest advantage. The demons of the beast always struck out when their powers reached the maximum; and as they prepared to release this massive amount of force, Xith attacked, dulling the release and usually destroying the recipient in the process. Yet as one disappeared, another would take its place. Closer and closer the hordes of death pushed. Xith's hands were a frenzy of scattered movements, tossing out a wave pattern of energy around them, hoping to hold the creatures at bay until his friends could all react. Ayrian had paused only a moment to seek the wildness from within. His talons became rapiers that tore through the opponents, his wings beat at the air, dancing him in and out of the ranks of the beast; and he quickly pursued Amir, until the two were poised directly in the midst of the enemy ranks.

"I gave you the chance to leave. You should have taken it!" said the wanderer as he appeared next to the startled wraith king.

"Master NooOOOOoooo," came the strangled cry from Mrak as he perished, instantaneously. The mighty wraith king had fallen like a child as Dalphan had devoured the negative energies of his life.

If there had been observers looking down from the gray canopy of the night sky, the great, domeless hall would have seemed a bowl filled with black pearls amongst which twinkled cheerless sapphires and hapless rubies, yet there were no such observers looking down. And to those that looked up, the hall seemed a shambles of fallen stone; and obscured by the dark horde in front of them, the gray sky was of little consequence. Each burst of evil, red against the protective shield that shimmered in ever-dwindling shades of yellow, brought evident pain to his face as the gifted guardian strained under the energies; and when he could no longer withstand them, the shield faltered for an instant and Noman fell to the ground in exhaustion.

"I cannot keep it up much longer under this pressure," he shouted to Xith. "You must eliminate the attacks to our rear!"

Expeditiously, Xith diverted his energies, and the change appeared to work, the shield strengthened and Noman sighed in relief. The beast and Amir locked eyes but could not close in on each other. Amir had waited centuries for the day when he would gain his revenge, as had the other. Amir increased his assault, wielding his blade with greater speed than he had ever attained before, and its edge, lethally-hewn, claimed many of the dark in the heated moments that followed. Having a difficult time keeping up with the pace Amir set, Ayrian was being pushed backward and downward by the horde of wraiths around him. The area he had been maneuvering in closed; and he was forced to the defensive, blocking and parrying, waiting for a moment when he could make a new thrust.

Behind the lines of wraiths a new force loomed closer. The hideously disfigured faces were the cause of Noman's agony and the reason his shield was growing less stable with each passing second. The magic of darkness was second nature to such creatures; they enjoyed a good fight and watching puny men squirm under their might. Their magic was black and evil, and extremely potent. Energies odd and ancient created explosions that rocked Noman's shield and sent him to his knees in recovery. This was the magic of the shadow demon, an ancient kin to the greater demons of the nether plane.

The marshaler of darkness and the grim warrior locked eyes again as they moved toward each other. Ayrian saw Amir's destination and became frantic; he had to stop him before they engaged one another. Amir's strength was needed elsewhere; the Beast could wait. Ayrian pumped his wings wildly. Raking one of the hags with his claw, he sent it tumbling into Amir, sending them both for a fall to one of the lower platforms. Dazed only for an instant, Amir stood and then he did a thing that momentarily surprised the eagle lord; he used hidden powers to carry him upward into the fray.

Noman's shield disintegrated as it was struck by blow upon blow, and he fell to the ground in agony. Fatigued and drawn, Noman recovered his feet. This time, it took considerable effort for him to restore his thoughts and reconstruct the protective shield. He wheeled around to face the demons as they stalked closer from the skies above; and raising a hand to them, he cursed their name. It was as the mystic did this that a spontaneous realization came to him—there were reasons for this dark night's visitation other than ending their four lives—under the strain of the battle, the thought slipped away.

A thunderous explosion broke through the cacophony of battle as the wanderer's rage struck one of the lesser demons, shattering its paltry shield with one passing thought; with the next he annihilated it. He set upon the greater and lesser demons each in turn; none could stand singly against him, and they were forced to turn their combined attentions toward him, leaving Xith and Noman with a moment's breathing space. Ayrian could no longer keep Amir and the Beast apart; their courses were set, and without the warrior's support, the wraiths closed in on his lone form. Fully encircled, Ayrian was too heavily engaged to seek them out. He now had his own concerns; yet in the distance, he heard them, the clang of steel striking steel resounded, adding a fresh, new sound to the din of the battlefield and, although Ayrian could no longer see either of them, he knew they battled because he could hear the tremendous blows.

Repeatedly Amir thrust out with his double-edged blade, the attack and counter-attacks made with the greatest dexterity and skill that he could manage. Whereas at first the creature could only hold his ground as Amir set upon him, the Beast seemed to feed off his attacks and grow stronger as Amir grew weaker. Now Amir was having to defend as often as attack and this confounded him. A presence edged closer and closer. Amir felt it approach in his mind. Yet just as the dark creature prepared to lash out at him from behind, it moved away. The Beast nodded his head in an onerous gesture and Amir understood—this was their fight; alone they would either be victorious or be defeated.

A gaping hole appeared suddenly in Noman's shield; he could see it in the image he held in the window of his mind except that he did not know how it had come to be. A pristine bolt of electricity that raised the hair on the back of his neck as it struck through the opening, nearly slicing his head off. He sighed heavily in relief; it had missed him. He quickly worked to restore the gap in the shield. The intensity of the concentration blurred his sight, and he did not see the shaman fall to the ground beside him. The bolt had caught his companion full in the chest, and the pain caused him to writhe on the ground and scream out. Arms that sought to lift crumbled beneath onerous weight, legs that should have hastened their support to their faltering companions went limp, and the stench of burning flesh flooded into air that had already been stagnated by a number of pungent odors, yet the resolute man did not succumb; he struggled, he resisted, he cried out.

Reacting to the screams, Ayrian turned about abruptly, folded his wings and dove. Driven on and sustained by the arousal of the magic within him, the shaman, obviously disoriented, found the tenacity to stand. He did so with apparent grogginess and sluggishness, motioning for Ayrian to find the source of the attack. From his vantage point, Ayrian quickly found it; the shimmering outline of the darkest of the forces of evil huddled all by itself in the corner was easily spotted. He had thought the dark ones fought with too much bravery; usually they held a cowardice in their eyes, and now that he knew the source of their bravery, he would end it. The shadow was too deeply involved in the melee to see the precipitous approach and the Gray Eagle Lord gained this advantage as he struck the creature from behind. Yet his talons had little effect on it; and hungrily it turned to look at him, raking him with cold, efficient claws as if to swat away a bothersome bug. The eagle lord's knee-jerk response was a high-pitched squeal that erupted from deep within him, the last sound to come to the field as the clamor of confusion and discord suddenly ebbed, and the arena grew seemingly still. Disconcerted, Noman looked up in awed surprise from his meditation, yet for the weary shaman the unsettling lull brought an unexpected repercussion— he staggered and fell, stumbling at first to his knees and then slipping to his haunches. He would rest a moment then rejoin the battle.

Perplexed by the stillness, Noman scoured the dark skies above them, searching futilely for a thing he would not find. Momentarily he fixed on the forms of Amir and the nameless beast; he knew the joy Amir must be feeling at the waiting's long end. Still, their fight was not the reason for the sudden shift in balance of power. His focus moved gradually to Ayrian and when he saw the shadow he understood, or at least he thought he did— the shadow demons had finally been summoned—the guardian was surely absent from the great gate, a thing that needed to be corrected if the forces of good were to survive. Ayrian had felt the icy hand slice downward and reach inside him, pulling with it in its retreat part of the energies of his life. A numbness radiated outward from the wound, tingling his clawed hand as it reached it, and then his whole winged arm fell limp at his side. Furious, knowing his time would be soon with only one arm to hold the shadow at bay, the proud lord, unwilling to accept defeat, lashed out more fervently, hoping he could lead the vile creature to where Xith could attack it, thus making it pay for its dark deed. Yet he did not know that the shaman was too weak to defend himself. All hope seemed lost, the forces of good would surely perish in their weakened state; and for an instant it seemed as if the dark forces were reveling in their sure victory. The ancient diviner was growing weak and his powers were near exhaustion; the powerful shaman was dreadfully wounded and might not be able to return to the battle; and the Gray Eagle Lord had just been dealt a crippling blow. Yet it was just then, when the battle seemed so near an end, that its outcome was forever changed and uncertainty returned to the field.

A cry rose through the air, long and powerful, the cry of blood.

"Brother, this is not your struggle!"

Four saw the figure that approached and knowing his name cursed, a multitude of darkness rejoiced. Noman now knew the one who held the guardian of the gate at bay.

"But it is—it is!" said the other.

Dalphan turned and met the cold stare of Sathar the Dark. Noman saw a test of time in the locked gazes.

"Why?" said the other with a voice deeply hurt and sad. "Why have you

turned your back on us, brother? You yourself made the pact and created the cycle."

Dalphan only answered with his own cold stare.

The voice set the shadow off balance and Ayrian seized the opportunity to lunge at it. He probed deep within the shadow with both his poised talons, severing the threads of the beast's negative energy from the inside out with a careful twisting of the energies that were within him. In a burst of evil yellow light the shadow winked from existence, hurled back to the plane it had been sent from. Ayrian inhaled a much-deserved breath of satisfaction; and then, as gravity took its course, he plummeted from the dark sky.

Two figures regarded each other for an instant more. Dalphan was the first to strike out. A sphere of brilliant blue-white light enshrouded his body, radiating, pulsating, when the power grew to its strongest in a dazzling array that when sent racing towards his foe turned night to day as opposing forces met in full fury. Seemingly meaningless, the other struggles around the crumbled dome ceased, and all eyes turned to watch the two with anticipation.

Sathar changed form and grew into a colossus, the shape of death incarnate, the shape of the most ancient demon the darkness had ever conjured. The demon seemed to smile as it enveloped Sathar and found life once again. Its misshapen form was a mass of wings and torso covered with a multitude of arms and legs, blocking out the light of the moon and stars from the sky while the tips of its leviathan wings beat against the edges of the dome sending shards of stone showering downward. With each such beat, a blast of gale-force winds kicked up dirt and rocks, even the large boulders that had toppled from the midsection of the great wall, into the air. The demon reached out with its barbed hands and buried Dalphan's small form within them, wresting the other's life with the weight of its grasp.

A howling, maddened cackle arose; shape-shifting was a skill given first to Dalphan. He easily transformed, slipping gradually through the demon's barbed hands. At first only a long, sinewy tail was visible, but then a large caped head eased upward. A giant serpent slithered from the demon's grasp, wrapping its way around the huge misshapen mass as it did so. With its deft coil, the serpent constricted while it wound its way up toward the great head of the demon. The snake hissed as it stood poised ready to strike, jaws spread wide, exposing its heinous fangs. A mocking laugh issued from the fiend and again it changed forms, shifting into the image of beauty and love in its purest form.

Dalphan looked into the eyes of his beloved and although he knew it was not her, he could not strike. The head of the serpent took on an inhuman face and tears issued from its inhuman eyes. Slowly, the face gathered mass, shifting back and forth between features, until it stopped and focused. The countenance Dalphan chose was not that of a terrestrial being, nor was it a creature of darkness, but that of the All-Father himself. The dark forces cowered in awe; their leader was so unnerved that he regained his true form. Dalphan's macabre demeanor drifted away and his mood turned to joy as he crushed the life from his brother; yet the dark one would not be defeated so easily. He knew his time here was spent—in another place and time, he could continue the struggle. He licked the saliva dripping from his lips and bit down upon the serpent, releasing the force of his soul upon Dalphan. Raw power exploded in the air, severing what remained of the dome and its supporting walls. In a flash of overbearing light, the two vanished, and in his mind Noman heard the clatter of the gate, a low, grinding rumble, as it snapped shut.

Slowly, very slowly, those assembled dishearteningly rejoined the attack; the forces of darkness were trapped now on this plane. The Beast and Amir found each other once again. They paused momentarily to let each other regather their wits; neither would take advantage of an unfair situation. This was a fight of honor between them. During the long struggle they had come to know each other; they were not much different. The child who had chosen light and the one who had chosen darkness had grown to respect each other.

Alone, Ayrian, Xith, and Noman stood on the platform and waited. Their thoughts wandered momentarily to the fallen form of a small boy, which lay partially buried beneath the rubble around them. The dark forces besieged them again. Although their number had considerably dwindled since their first attack, their glee was now disenchanted, and they could no longer draw upon the powers of that other dark world. Noman stole a moment of hesitation to touch a healing hand to Ayrian, enabling him to return to the sky upon fleet wings. Like Xith, he only had the power of binding, yet this was all that was necessary. Afterwards he looked to the shaman. Only three of the demons remained and with unspoken approval Xith lashed out, immediately taking the first's shield, which was weak and did not last long. The others quickly retaliated. Their energies buzzed against Noman's skillfully balanced shield while he waited for the attack to fade so he could join Xith. In a surge of power, together Xith and Noman destroyed the last two demons; then, it seemed, only the wraiths remained in opposition.

Ayrian, in spite of the only partially healed wound, was taking his toll on the wraiths; however, it was clear that without aid he would not last. The numbers would soon overwhelm him. Xith and Noman came quickly to his aid. The diminished numbers of wraiths could not withstand the combined attacks, and in defeat they were forced to retreat. Another force remained hidden and obscure in the shadows. Only one of their kind had fallen, but they were determined not to rejoin the dispute. They had been promised things that could not possibly be delivered now, and they no longer feared their master's wrath. They had freedom if only they could escape, and escape is what they sought. They slipped into the stillness of the night. They did not howl at their newfound freedom, but they did gloat in it. The nameless beast readily followed; victory or defeat would have to wait.

The dark wraiths turned back on Ayrian for a brief moment to surmise the strength of the weakened soul. A captured soul to feed upon would be a prize to relish, yet without guidance they were hesitant, and it was this hesitation that defeated them. Cries of surprise and agony rang out as the light of early morning dawned. Ayrian pursued the routed creatures until he was sure they would not return, then slowly he drifted back to the platform. His body ached with fatigue and pain as he slumped down beside the battered shaman. The wise diviner touched restraining hands to the weary two as they sought to rise upon unsteady limbs.

"This is their fight," he whispered, yet even as Noman spoke these words, the strange battle was coming to an end.

The dark figure fled, leaving behind a confused Amir.

"Am I then finished here?" asked Amir, turning to greet the diviner's eyes with an expectant stare, "Is it time?"

"No, not yet, my old friend. This was only a stage in the momentous struggle in which we play out only a small part, yet that part is not yet complete," replied Noman.

"What of Dalphan and of the boy?"

Noman held back a show of emotion from his weary face. Sweat mixed with soot trickled down his cheeks in thick lines that outlined the scowling and troubled countenance. "Come, we must go. The city is as weary as I, and as I have said, this is merely the beginning. We have other concerns before us now, chief among which are rest and recuperation."

Noman looked up to the dark sky. "Hurry now. Sathar may return at any time."

"Sathar is defeated," said Amir.

"Trust me when I say the fight has only begun and that Sathar lives— because he does. Dalphan fought a projection of his dark brother's will nothing more." Noman urged Xith and Ayrian to their feet, then turned back to Amir as he cast the orb to the ground. "Hurry now," he told them. "There is little time and much to do."

The four stepped into the spinning circle of light and disappeared.

8

The training grounds were thoroughly saturated, covered from end to end with what might have looked like thousands of tiny ants from high above. A viewing platform had been erected and raised high. It was from here that Valam surveyed the lines of riders, hunters, pikemen, swordsmen, bowmen, and shield bearers.

"How goes the training, Prince Valam?" asked Chancellor Van'te.

"It goes well. Within the week we shall be ready to depart. The troops will have more than sufficient training by then; besides the winter snows are gone and they grow more restless with each passing day."

"Yes, I can see," answered Chancellor Van'te as he looked down at the group occupied in a match of crossed swords.

"It is all in fun. I think I will go join them. It is time I showed Brother Seth how to really handle a weapon."

"My lord, which is Ylsa's formation?" asked the chancellor in a fluid, casual manner.

"Third column from the—" Valam stopped, catching himself in a blunder.

Van'te held back a laugh as the prince descended from the platform and crossed the field to join Evgej and Seth's group.

"There you are, Chancellor Van'te," said Keeper Martin as he appeared at the top of the balcony. "Father Jacob and I were just discussing a few things. We want your opinion also. I think we should go back to the planning room."

Chancellor Van'te sent for horses and the two, with a small escort, returned to Quashan'. The keeper enjoyed the short stint in the saddle although he would have preferred to return in the same manner he had arrived. It would have been quicker and much more efficient.

During the brief ride, Van'te talked with the keeper only sporadically; mostly he pondered his own concerns. He was glad that Prince Valam had come home although he didn't like the idea of his leaving so soon. He had been silently siding with Isador and King Andrew. It was time for the prince to marry and settle down. He had held high hopes that Valam would find a suitable wife when he returned, but now the plans of courtship and wedding would have to be put on hold.

The two walked quietly toward the great hall, which had been converted to a planning room. A man of great wisdom, the chancellor now sought to anticipate what Father Jacob and Keeper Martin wished to discuss. He plotted his options and his responses accordingly. He noted how strangely quiet the palace was for mid-day. It was not the center of the activities in South Province any more. Most of the pages and guards had been dispatched to the camp to keep everything in order there. The chancellor sighed. The majority of those that remained in the palace were servants that tended to cleaning and upkeep. He rather missed the bustling days. The camp was too disorderly for him. In the palace, he could maintain control and do so in an orderly fashion.

The chancellor could see from the dark circles under Keeper Martin's eyes that he had not slept in a very long time; along with the fatigue, a rigid mask of worry had also set in. When they reached the hall, Van'te saw that Father Jacob did not look much better; if it were possible, he looked worse.

"Why the glum moods? Is it truly that bad here?" joked Van'te.

"No, chancellor, your hospitality has been exquisite. We are having a crisis. Oh, how do I start? Let me just say this bluntly. The situation we are dealing with is very grave. We thought it best we told you here in private," began Father Jacob, pausing to take a sip from a glass of water.

"Go on," said Chancellor Van'te, eager to hear what Jacob had to say.

"Last night Keeper Martin received a dream message from the Council of Keepers, the second. It was pretty unclear in parts but quite vivid in others. Many things are changing. They mentioned great shifts in power."

"Shifts in *power*?" Chancellor Van'te couldn't quite follow what Jacob was saying.

"From the Father and the Mother. I have felt it from the Father, and the priestesses of the Mother sent word to the council that the Mother was distressed."

Jacob took another sip from his glass; the liquid trickling down his throat soothed its soreness.

"What do you mean distressed?" interrupted Van'te again, his face quite livid with anger, "Why wasn't I told sooner?"

"There is more. Please be patient. I have not told Prince Valam yet either."

"So why did Keeper Martin only come for me?"

"Chancellor, please, I know you are angry. That is understandable, but we had to be sure that what we told you was correct. As you can see, I haven't slept for many days.

"Two nights ago I felt the Father cry out. I have never felt such great emotions. They were quite clear, as if something were tearing him apart; then they changed suddenly and calmed. Something terrible has come to pass. The portent has come. I can feel it.

"The darkness has returned to Kir."

Van'te gasped as Jacob uttered the forbidden word, and at the same time it flooded his thoughts with memories. For a moment the implications of Jacob's words were lost as he focused solely on the word and not what Jacob had just finished telling him; then it clicked and he understood. "It is no more?"

"So it seems. We may be too late in journeying to the Eastern Reaches, but we must try."

"How soon must we leave?"

"As soon as possible."

"That will take a great deal of work, yet I think Prince Valam and I can get everything together," spoke Van'te, adding, "now if you'll excuse me I need to start."

"Wait! Chancellor Van'te, there is something else," yelled Keeper Martin.

"What is it?" responded Van'te impatiently.

"Well, it is a delicate matter," spoke Father Jacob, motioning for the chancellor to step back into the room and close the door.

"Yes?" said Van'te, his eyes flashing; the chancellor was naturally an impatient person. Time was very important to him. He couldn't stand to waste even a moment of its preciousness.

"It is Prince Valam," replied Martin.

Chancellor Van'te drummed his fingers on the edge of the table, waiting for the keeper to hurry up and tell him what he was going to say.

"We do not feel it is the proper time for him to leave the kingdom. We feel he should stay here."

"*We?* I can feel something," added Jacob.

Van'te understood now why Keeper Martin had been slow to speak his mind and why they had brought him here alone. He felt foolish for his flippant attitude.

"I am sorry; I am often impetuous. It is just that I am overzealous," said Van'te.

"We know how you are. There is nothing wrong with that."

"You and your brother are much alike," added Jacob with a chuckle as he pictured Yi in this situation.

"I will talk to Prince Valam," said Van'te, "yet you both need to promise me something."

"Certainly, if there is any way we can help."

"Yes, actually there is. You two go and get some sleep. I'll need you at your fullest over these next days."

Jacob offered no arguments, yet Martin stared, dreary eyes and all, at the chancellor as the two departed. Chancellor Van'te sent for runners and his page. He had many things to prepare before this day was out. He sent the first runner to find Prince Valam; and afterwards, he dispatched several others to spread the news throughout the camp and to bring word to the ship captains.

Van'te didn't have much time to consider how he wanted to direct the conversation with Prince Valam before the page returned, panting heavily from the run. Van'te dismissed him in quick order with one last errand for the day, just as the prince and several others arrived. Valam could see from the disorder in the room and the wild look in Van'te's eyes that something drastic was amiss. He signaled for the guards to close the door behind him.

"We came as soon as we could. The page sounded so urgent. What is it?" asked Valam.

Chancellor Van'te quickly explained, touching only lightly on what had been said, and moved on to talk about stepping up the preparations for departure.

"Will you have enough time to get everything in order?"

Captain Vadan Evgej eyed the chancellor. "We will most certainly try!" he said.

Valam added, "We will do more than try; we will do it!" and then they each scrambled off.

"Prince Valam?" called out Van'te after him, "Could you wait a moment please."

Prince Valam detected the tone of Van'te's voice and grew concerned.

"What is wrong?"

The chancellor quickly calculated all the ways he could best explain to Valam the gravity of the situation. He thought of just telling him bluntly what Martin had said although he knew Valam well enough to know that he had to put the matter delicately. The words he chose never reached his lips. Within the upturned, waiting eyes, he saw a thing he would relish for years to come, the impatient longing of youth.

"Prince Valam, do not forget to check the ships in port."

Valam promised he would not and raced after the others.

"Prince Valam?" called out the chancellor again, as he stepped into the hall.

"Yes," came the distant response.

Van'te hesitated again.

"Did I tell you Isador is returning to Imtal Palace? Which means the—"

"—wedding plans are off," finished Valam happily, ending his retreat.

"Yes, she has plans for another now."

"*Adrina?*" asked Valam turning to face the chancellor, staring down the long hall.

"So it would seem," cast back the chancellor.

Men were sent to gather equipment and food stores and to load the ships. Confusion, which took a concerted effort to quell, spread throughout the camp. All were eager to leave; however, they had not thought it would be so soon. Once they were on the ships there would be no turning back.

Captain Cagan drank in the night air from the sea. He had departed with the first detachment sent to the coast. It had been so long since he had sailed. He longed to be back on the open water. Thinking of the sea reminded him of home, which seemed suddenly closer. He had come to know these people and respect their ways. He counted them as friends. Still, there was no substitute for his own home.

"Captain Cagan, thinking of home?" came the voice from the shore.

"Yes, Brother Seth, I am." Cagan shouted back.

"Me too!" intoned Seth quietly, "Me too."

Seth jumped into one of the long boats that were shuttling back and forth from the shore.

"She is a fine ship, Captain Cagan. Looks almost like—" shouted Seth as he climbed to the low deck.

"My old ship. Yes. A friend at the shipyard wanted to know how we designed our ships. I drew him up some diagrams. Our ships are not much different. The hull shapes are almost identical."

Seth shot a quick salutation to the oarsman and then yawned a heavy, stretching yawn. The making of ships didn't interest him as it did Cagan, yet he wouldn't interrupt; his friend's love for ships was clear. Cagan babbled on for awhile with Seth adding little to the conversation. He stared out across the black waters, looking to a distant shore. Thoughts of home filled his mind.

"I knew it! I knew I would find you two here," said Valam as he and Evgej emerged from the opposite side of the deck.

"All clear," he shouted down to the oarsman.

"All clear, cast off," was the return response.

"All should be set soon; isn't this fantastic?"

Seth nodded and Cagan returned to his talk of ships. Valam smiled as he crossed to Seth, joining him in his fixed stare out across the waters. He absorbed the peacefulness of the waves and the setting of the sun, a red-orange ball of fire one-third submerged beneath the dark waters.

Valam didn't invalidate the grand illusion with clear thoughts. He relaxed for a moment, allowing his mind to wander freely. "Check the ships in port indeed," he muttered to himself, wondering what the old chancellor was up to.

As he surveyed the ship, he saw a glowing shimmer shoot up the main mast. The soft golden glow lasted only a moment but the way the light moved reminded him of what had happened when Eldrick had entered the Sentinel tree. *Couldn't be, could it?* He thought to himself as he stared up at the mast. The thought was lost though as Seth and Cagan urged him up to the high deck. From the high deck near the ship's wheel, the trio stared out into the night and wondered what the morrow would bring.

9

Adrina walked through the garden lost in thought, as she did often now. Many thoughts crossed her mind, each seeming to blow in and out with a fresh breeze. She walked until she came to the white gazebo in the center of the garden and rested a bit. She had not felt well lately and grew tired easily. Her skin was milky white and her eyes held a pinkish haze. Father Francis blamed it on her not eating though she insisted she had been eating.

Pain hit her suddenly and she doubled over. She began to cry out as she coughed up blood once more. The tiny dragon she had named Tnavres dropped from her shoulder and licked the blood hungrily. "Stop!" she called out to the beast. "Follow, hurry!"

Tnavres hopped back onto her shoulder. She waved a finger to scold him. "Naughty, Tnavres," she said, "Bad dragon."

Dizzy and weak, slowly she staggered back to her room. She would not tell Father Francis about this. She hoped she could make it back to her chamber without him or any of the servants spotting her. The walk seemed overly long and arduous. It was all she could do to hold herself upright. She was so very tired; her body desperately needed sleep. Everything spun suddenly and she grabbed out at the wall, using it as a support.

Tnavres flapped his wings rapidly from his perch atop her shoulder. He was as agitated as she was disoriented. Without warning he launched from her shoulder.

She reached out to catch him but as she did this, he turned about and locked his jaws around her hand. His teeth plunged inward; the flesh of her hand turned to stone. As she stumbled and fell against the wall, she gripped her forearm and squeezed with all her might as if this alone could stop the progression.

"No, not again," she whispered as she clutched her arm.

"Yes, again," came the voice. "You don't listen."

"But I have listened and done all you asked. I gave you it all. What more do you want? What more?"

"You know what more. What must I do to convince you?"

"Never," she cried out.

In her mind's eye, Adrina saw the Dragon King, his great wings spread wide and his great clawed hands reaching out, enveloping her. "To live, you must. It will only take a moment and then it will be done. You must not fight; you must accept. Do you understand?"

Adrina started to respond. Pain swept through her body. She coughed up blood. "You are a liar!" she shouted.

"Not me," said the Dragon King. "This is not my doing. Hurry now or it will be too late."

Adrina writhed and convulsed on the floor. "Make it stop," she whimpered.

"Only you, Adrina Alder, can make it stop. Do what I've asked and it will be done."

The pain sought to sweep her away. "Yes," she shouted out, "I'll do whatever you ask."

"So be it," said the Dragon King and with the saying, the one became the many and the dragon flock took flight.

On the floor beside her, Tnavres released his grip on her hand. He jumped up onto her leg, cocked his head to the side as if listening to something or someone unseen. With his head, he lifted up her shirt then he faded into her, leaving only his mark upon her skin.

Adrina's eyes went wide as the pain left her. She stood unsteadily then hurried down the hall. When she reached her room, she crawled into bed and soon fell asleep. She was so tired and her bed was so warm and soothing. A convulsion sent a shock wave through her body that forced her to consciousness. Rubbing her head as it throbbed, she made her way to the basin near the bed. Her hand trembled violently as she poured a cup of water and raised it to her lips. She spilled most of it onto the floor. The cool water was momentarily soothing to her throat and stomach. She dipped a cloth into the basin and touched it to her forehead, groping her way back to bed. A cough sent her into another seizure and she vomited up the water. Afterwards she grew sleepy again and fell back to sleep.

A familiar sound drifted into her thoughts, a voice that had soothed her through many childhood illnesses. The voice of the one who had recently left her, Isador, whispering to her that everything would be all right. She wondered if she were dreaming, but then the voice streamed into her consciousness again, soft and pleasant, nurturing.

"I am sorry, Izzy," she said, momentarily slipping into the familiar little girl's voice that the presence of her nanny stirred. "I didn't mean for you to have to return to Imtal. I'm getting better really. I'll be fit in no—"

"I don't think so. You just rest for awhile. I will be back momentarily," Myrial said, cutting Adrina short. She did not have the heart to tell her that she was not Isador.

Adrina rapidly dropped off. She dreamed of Valam and Seth. All the arguments and fun times they had had together. She missed them both. Images played in her unconscious for a time, and then she entered a pleasant deep slumber. She had only been asleep for a couple of hours, or so it seemed, when she was awakened. The voice sounded so urgent, and so very distant.

"Wake up, princess, wake up!" shouted Myrial.

To Adrina, it seemed it was Isador who shook her again and again and wiped her face with a wet, soothing cloth.

"Please, Adrina. Wake up," begged the girl.

Adrina didn't want to wake up; she still was so tired. She wanted to sleep.

"Wha-a-at?" she asked groggily.

"Come quick, princess!"

"Whaaat isss itt?" asked Adrina through a yawn.

"It is King Andrew; hurry."

Thoughts of sleep were suddenly chased away. Adrina jumped out of bed, pulling a robe around her as she raced out the door and down the hall to her father's chamber.

Father Francis and many others were gathered around his bedside when she arrived. The priests of the Father led by Francis were chanting words in the holy tongue; and from the level of their tone, she knew something was amiss. Her father smiled as he saw her face. He waved at the priests to fend them off and to end their unnerving chanting.

She quickly knelt beside his bed, taking his hand as she did so. She asked Father Francis what was wrong, but he only answered by shaking his head. She tightly clasped her father's hand and burst into tears.

"Don't go, father, please!" begged Adrina, "I love you!"

King Andrew brushed the tears from her eyes and held her hand. "Don't be frightened, my child," he spoke weakly, "it will be fine, just fine."

Andrew bit back the pain that was welling up inside him. He coughed and spit blood onto the pillow beside him. Father Francis jumped to his sire's side, attempting to push Adrina away, so he could continue the healing rights.

"No, please, no!" screamed Adrina.

"She will stay," said Andrew in a voice that was scarcely audible.

Father Francis released Adrina and she raced back to her father's side.

"Stay with me!" whispered Adrina, turning Andrew's words back around.

A sparkle touched his eyes as he took her hand again. "Send word to Valam to return at once," he said, pulling her close to him as he whispered in her ear, "I love you, my daughter, you are my pride and Valam and Calyin, my joy. I go now to her. She's waited so long."

Andrew's voice faded off as he spoke, the pain becoming too much for him. He squeezed Adrina's hand tightly and then sighed a gasp of relief, holding his composure even at the end.

The priests started to chant loudly, wild in their requests to the Father to spare their monarch's life. Father Francis even offered his own life in place of Andrew's, but the Father would not accept his offer. Sadly the chants shifted from pleas to the cry for the dead, a song of mourning.

King Andrew's last words to Adrina had been words of love for his kingdom and his family. Adrina was swept with tears. She cried out to the Great Father, but received no answer. Attempting to soothe her, Father Francis embraced her. Adrina ran away screaming as he touched her. She ran until she came to her room, where she slammed and bolted the door.

10

A small group of weary survivors stood in the midst of the gap in the great Northern Range where the trail that cut its way up Solstice Mountain ended, and the great trail that spread through the gap converged on several others smaller than itself. Staring heavenward, they watched the mantel of haze dissipate. And for the first time eyes were allowed to gaze upon the lofty peak from so far below.

Those watching knew with certainty that the City of the Sky was no more. As they had chased the hushed veil of twilight down the mountain, Noman had reconsidered a thought that had briefly passed through his mind in the heat of the battle; a force beyond Sathar the Dark was at work here playing a guarded game with the balance of power. He wondered who or what it was that played such a twisted game and what sort of amusement it brought, realizing with certainty that this first challenge had been just that—a challenge meant to divert attention away from something greater. But what was it? Momentarily satisfied by the sense that something would be revealed soon, Noman shrugged his shoulders and cast the thoughts away. After all, there were more pressing matters to consider and the shaman's voice could not have caught him at a more opportune moment.

"Come!" said Xith weakly, "My home is not far from here. We can rest there and heal our wounds." Xith's voice trailed off as he finished and he slumped to the ground. His face, beaded heavily with perspiration, was deathly pale.

Ayrian was the first to his side, at first attempting to help his weary companion to his feet. Yet as the shaman's hands fell away, his tunic, lacerated and charred in a wide circle around the chest and shoulder area, revealed a large patch of scorched and blistered flesh beneath.

"What of the boy?" asked Xith, his last words as he slipped into unconsciousness. He had seen the form of the boy fall and the will of the wanderer rise.

"Now is the time to tend to wounds," said Noman, "there is no hurry now; morning comes." His voice rose at the last with an air of hope.

"The shadows," whispered Ayrian, his words at first in response to the diviner and then to the shaman. "He is no more."

"Shadows fade in the sunlight," whispered Noman, returning the foreboding tone that Ayrian had used with equal fervor. "Sit," he ushered, indicating that Ayrian, too, should rest.

"I am fine, old one, tend to Xith," said Ayrian, despite the deep gouge stemming from elbow to shoulder.

Noman and Amir worked long to clean and bind the wounds. Xith's injury continued to fester no matter what they did; the flesh all around it was seared, shock had set in, and they feared the worst for the shaman. The Gray Eagle Lord's shoulder wound was by far less severe; and in time, he would regain the use of his arm and the attached wing though it would be sore for some time and would have to be re-worked into shape. Still, he would most certainly recover.

Noman sent Amir to cut down two saplings and strip the leaves and branches from them. With them, he formed a stretcher of sorts, in which they could carry Xith. Once it was secure, they placed Xith on it. The next step was to find the place Xith spoke of, and to do this Noman would have to connect with the shaman's weakened mind. He touched a soft hand to Xith's forehead and probed his mind, searching through thoughts that flowed to him without resistance until he found what he was looking for, the hidden entrance to the fallen city of Ywentir, a place lost to most save the Watcher and now Noman.

Ywentir was a place much like the Cloud City; both were distant images from the past, times when great secrecy prevailed, times when there had been so much need and so little hope, times when sanctuaries had been a desperate necessity yet were now only faint, distant memories. The mystical city had been one of the last strongholds of the peoples of the northern realms, and in fact had been the last stronghold of the Keepers of the Watch eons ago. The travelers would be safe there as long as they could reach it before the arrival of night. He knew, as they all did, the dark forces were by no means defeated. They had just begun the challenge. The minions of darkness were many, unlike those of good, who numbered few, and they would be set back only temporarily by the night's proceedings.

The three, shouldering the burden of Xith's still form, made their way along the path that would carry them through the mountains toward the land of the North though not through it, for the northern lands were oddly separated, segregated by the great mountains themselves. Two great spines of the Northern Range divided the land into three disparate tracts. There had once been many who knew the paths and tunnels that connected the lands, but alas no more. Noman would have to rely on the information that he had gleaned from the shaman's mind, for even he was not privy to the secrets that the northlands held.

Like the three vastly different lands and the three vastly different peoples the land held, there had once been three cities that symbolized the three peoples, sisters in spirit, separated by the land forever.

Ywentir, Tsitadel', Aurentid, repeated Noman in his mind. During the Blood Wars, the secrecy of the northerners proved to be the bane of the dark forces, yet even such a powerful pact of silence had not saved the northern lands or those that fled to it in fruitless attempts to escape the ravages of a war that spread across the continent like a monstrous plague.

Aurentid had been the first to fall and nothing of it remained except shattered walls and piles of rubble; Ywentir with its protective maze had succumbed by a different means than its ill-fated sister though it too had eventually fallen; yet as Noman well knew, for he had been there, Tsitadel' had never fallen, though its survival had been by the barest of margins and through means perhaps darker than even the dark forces would have levied against it.

Ayrian stopped cold, his keen senses perceiving something that the others did not. He stared up at the mountain and the sky, cocking his head in his odd way so that it faced the direct opposite of its normal position. His vision, the vision of the great eagle, was far greater than the others, so what he saw eluded them. He pointed to a tiny speck of light far up the mountain, which gained intensity as it drew nearer.

Amir took a step forward while the others held still. They waited and watched. The litter was set gently to the ground and the noble warrior lifted his weapon from its sheath with deft hands. The glowing ball of heavenly light was almost upon them; and, as Noman sensed no malicious intent, he gestured to Amir to return his blade to its sheath. Amir did.

Ayrian could almost make out a shape inside the shimmering yellow light, two shapes actually, and then when the others began to see the shapes, he saw the outlines of a man of early years and of a woman whose hand he held. A few yards from where the company stood, the ball of light stopped and after settling to the mountain's side, those within stepped out.

The two, the man of early years and the woman whose hand he still held, turned to wave goodbye to the strange glowing ball of light as it lifted into the sky. The woman appeared to be an angel, for no one else could have been so beautiful, so perfect. She had long, golden brown hair and a darkly tanned body. She wore a cloth dress, sheer and white, clearly accentuating her sublime body, which, although it left little to the imagination, did not taint the pureness she emitted—an impure thought would have been impossible.

Amir stared at her in open admiration of her beauty. The young man they all knew. He released the woman's hand and walked over to them. He knelt beside Xith, his head bent in prayer. The others had known the youngster in a different form. The one that stood before them was no longer riddled with latent power, nor was it that of a boy; it had changed. Vilmos was clear of the wild magic, or so it seemed. He was his own person once again, yet it was as though he had raced through time in years instead of hours since the Wanderer's fall.

The woman approached Xith. She spoke in hushed tones with a melodic, captivating voice. She touched his wound and began to chant loudly, her words flowing like music. When she stopped, she put a hand to his eyes and said, "He will rest now and will surely recover soon."

Momentary disbelief passed over Ayrian. He touched a hand to the shaman's brow; the fever had, indeed, broken and color was returning to his ashen features. He stared up at Noman, who had also gathered near, his great round eyes spread wide. The power of true healing was granted primarily to the priestesses, so Noman was sure that she must be one of the priestesses of the Mother, truly a magnificent gift.

She looked to Ayrian and smiled, a delicate smile that matched her delicate touch. She chanted a different song than she had sung for the shaman, a sweet, short song, which, when she finished, left Ayrian completely healed. Ayrian thanked her for her kindness and then she looked to the others, each in turn. Amir radiated as their eyes caught. They stared into each other's eyes for a moment.

Emotions were kindled in Amir that it seemed he had not felt the whole of his life. She smiled and then simply turned to Noman, who was the last. When she was sure they were all healthy, she took Vilmos by the hand and wordlessly led him away, along the trail.

All eyes were on Vilmos as the two walked away. They wanted to know what had happened and why he was here. They had thought him lost in the battle and now here he stood with them. Noman was quick to perceive the hand of the Father; Amir was not. Amir picked up one end of the litter and Noman the other, and they set off after Vilmos.

Noman wasn't surprised as the woman led them through places only he and Xith should know. He had seen shadings of this path, though he had not seen where it would lead them. He accepted the circle of life. Simply knowing Vilmos' time was not yet spent was good enough for him. The other troubled him. In the visions he had never seen the face or form of their new companion, only the outlines of where someone would be in the path.

He cleared his mind, following Amir as he took a step, focusing his thoughts inward, searching for the facts that eluded him. He saw only the others along the path he chose and when he searched further the vision ended. A peculiar image remained, a mark over the young man's visage that he had never seen before; and although he scoured his thoughts, he could not find its origin. Perplexed, he trudged on.

The city was not far; however, the journey was over rough terrain and along some dark paths. Weary, Noman took a reprieve from carrying Xith and now Amir and Vilmos performed the task. Xith was still soundly sleeping when at last they emerged from the darkness; and steep walls of stone rose on either side of them as they entered a narrow, sequestered canyon.

A whole new world opened up to them as they walked among the new shadows formed by the dull light filtering down from a sun that seemed so tiny and so high above them. The coveted entrance they sought was midway up the cliff wall on the far side of the canyon and with luck they would reach it safely before the arrival of the first whispers of dusk. The path, though it had apparently once been worn smooth, was uneven and largely overgrown. Carrying the litter forced frequent stops, and progress through the deep canyon was slow.

Vilmos was quite intrigued by the gorge. Carved out of solid rock, its origin seemed a mystery to him. As he thought of this and reflected upon the recent happenings, his life seemed quite similar to the heartless rock that surrounded them, going from stable to unstable, swimming in and out of some unseen revelation in directions unknown and seemingly coerced by nature itself.

Early afternoon brought heavier shadows to the canyon and with it came an unsettling chill. The air, which had scarcely stirred before, calmed as they approached the stark face of a blunt stone wall, which, though still several hours away, was clearly visible now. The shadows gradually blackened until true darkness settled upon them; elsewhere night was some hours away, but within the ravine, night had already begun. A sense of urgency quickened their pace, and the stops became less frequent and then ceased completely as the companions dashed for the safety that seemed just within their grasp.

Ayrian took flight despite his need to heal, ridding the skies of imagined specters. The race for safety was on. A dull twinge of pain swept through Vilmos' mind. Warily, he cast his eyes to the heavens, seeking to look beyond the blank, dark walls. A voice within him shouted out. It whispered, "Only seven remain," though Vilmos did not listen. That part of him was lost.

The canyon wall was only a few hundred yards away now. Sensing the encroaching darkness, the six ran at a full pace. Amir and Noman temporarily shouldered the burden of the litter, jostling the injured passenger. A dark shape passed overhead and all cringed, although it was only Ayrian settling to the ground.

The entrance to the city lay some three hundred feet off the canyon floor, barricaded by a great stone. Only a carefully trained eye could discern the outline of the door from the dark stone of the wall, yet two did see it. Without rope and grapple, there was no visible way to make the climb—that is, if any sort of grapple would have held in the sheer rock face. The only way up would be to fly, or to levitate. Noman knew this. Yet he didn't know if the newcomer could perform the feat, for although a strange aura surrounded her, he perceived no flow of magic.

As he contemplated this, she began to rise into the air. Ayrian gently buffeted the same cold air with his wings, slowly, steadily moving up the cliff wall with Amir behind him; together they ferried Xith. Noman directed the magic within with a quietly intoned word of focusing and floated up after the others. The only one that remained on the canyon floor was Vilmos.

"What's the matter?" yelled Noman down to him.

"I don't know how to fly!"

Noman chuckled.

"Wait there; we'll return for you."

Glumly, Vilmos waited in the darkness. Elsewhere night had finally arrived. He felt things coming to life in the arrival of night and it sent a trickle of unease down his back. He watched as Amir pressed his weight and might against the great stone and then the voices and partially perceived figures disappeared. He was alone again. He began turning around and around in tiny circles brought on by nervousness and agitation and the very real images of his imagined specters sneaking up on him.

Icy cold hands reached out of the darkness and grasped his arm. Vilmos started and screamed out, pulling away from the deft fingers.

Skilled in the use of the voice, Noman reached out with it to the young man's ears. *"Calm yourself!"*

The commanding voice held no influence over Vilmos, and he trembled as he was yanked upwards. The gray shadow of the wall passed before his eyes and the dim presence of distant stars seemed to grow suddenly closer. And then all movement stopped. Vilmos felt the coarseness of stone against his skin as he brushed up against it. Noman led the way into the recess, a small, low cave.

Vilmos' eyes seemed only then to adjust to the darkness. He saw Amir, his large proportions barely accommodated. He was forced to crouch almost to a crawling position; hunched over like that, he looked suddenly larger than life. Xith, still on the litter, lay next to the opposite wall. Ayrian was at his side. And the other stood just in front of him and to the left, the dull outline of a tunnel behind her.

The tunnel ran from the cave deep into the unknown mountain, dead-ending in a circular cavern of immense size and height. Here, Amir breathed in heartily as he stretched to his full height. Only one pathway led into or out of the cave, the one they entered through, and they were stuck or so it appeared. Hesitating only momentarily, Noman gestured that they should proceed to the far side of the large cavern, and they did. It was a short trek compared to the long one through the previous tunnel. Vilmos was just about to grab Noman about the shoulders and warn him that he was about to walk into the shadowed wall, when the other reached his hand out and moved it through the dark stone of the wall. Vilmos flushed and started. A crafty smile lit the old one's face as he turned back to Vilmos. The illusion of the blank wall, which his special skills allowed him to see through easily, had a portal in it that led into an adjacent shaft. This new shaft, cut almost smooth and round, not jagged and rough, was one that was clearly made by hand, not formed by nature.

The group paused so Amir could return to the entrance to replace its blocking stone, allowing only a tiny slit to be seen from the outside again.

Once the stone was in place and Amir had returned, Noman conjured a mystical flame to guide them. The odd, magical flame was the darkest, deepest blue at its heart, which as it radiated outward lessened until it was a brilliant, fine white light that was solely directed outward and forward, shining like a blossoming beacon.

A series of tunnels that twisted and connected and circled crisscrossed the main corridor at different levels, forming a maze that could have swallowed them forever if they had not known where they were going. The maze had but one simple rule: a number of markers were spread out in the grottoes and galleries they would come across—chambers, caverns, rooms, and tunnels, those naturally formed and those hand-hewn. The advice of the markers was poor, as they all pointed in a particular direction, which would only get one deeper into the catacombs. The markers always occurred at crossings and the correct route was to follow only the corridor whose entrance began farthest from the marker, a distance that often had to be paced off.

From the first passage they turned left, then right, and then followed a series of descending passageways twisting this way and that. Noman did all the necessary pacing for measurements. Vilmos counted the crossways and chambers though no one else apparently did. He wondered what could have been so valuable that it needed to be so fiendishly guarded. They veered left and then straight for awhile, then right, through to a shaft ending at a large set of double doors. Noman uttered the simple command, "Dver Otkrys!" and the doors opened inwards on a puff of air. Once they had all entered, the doors gently closed. They stood within a smoothly carved hall that ran for several hundred yards before ending at another set of doors that opened inward easily without command as Noman gingerly pushed on them.

"Behold, the city of Ywentir," cried Noman.

And Vilmos' question was at last answered.

11

Adrina grew stronger during the next several days although she still felt unwell. She knew what was wrong with her though no one had told her. Isador had been distant from her these past days, not like her usual self. Everyone within the palace was so diffident, and the palace itself was sealed tight. Everywhere she went, two guards followed her. When she tried to eat, they stopped her until the food and drink had been thoroughly tasted. She felt like a prisoner in her own home.

From her bed, she stared towards the open sunlit window, though few rays came into her chamber. She sighed, resigned to wait for the summons to come to her door. The summons came and the door swung open and Isador came in.

As the door came to rest against the wall, Isador brought a breakfast tray, a breakfast that grew cold as it was tasted repeatedly. Adrina cast several dark grimaces at the guards before they retreated, and she was allowed to eat in peace. She had little appetite after they had been digging through her food, tasting this, sipping at that; yet she was hungry, so she ate.

Isador could tell something was troubling Adrina. Still, she waited without uttering a word until she had finished her meal. She picked up the tray of food and walked away silently. Adrina called out to Isador and looked her in the eyes.

"I want to hear it from you. Tell me please—"

"It is nothing," said Isador in a weak voice.

"Isador?" begged Adrina.

"I am not supposed to tell you, dear."

"You always tell me everything, Izzy. You are my best friend, right?" said Adrina.

"It is the poison I am concerned about," whispered Isador, slipping.

"*Poison?*"

"Poison," repeated the nanny. She said nothing further, for she knew she had said too much already.

"But—"

Loud hysterical yelling issuing from the hall stopped Adrina. The message the man was screaming was clear, yet somehow strange. Adrina whispered the words in her mind, "The fallen have returned, the fallen have returned." What did it mean?

Adrina rushed to the door to investigate, but the guards stopped her.

"Isador, please!"

Adrina continued to beg even though Isador was weeping. Finally Isador yielded to the pleas, agreeing only if the guards accompanied them. Adrina's face lit up with a crafty grin. She wasn't quite sure which direction the man had come from although she was confident that if there were trouble, she would find it.

She followed a group of guards as they rushed toward the western wing until she came to a place where she was halted. A group of guards blocked the end of the hall and would not let her or anyone else pass. The sergeant was quite polite in his refusal; Adrina was outraged nonetheless.

"I order you to let me pass!" repeated Adrina.

"I cannot," said the guard again politely.

He dispatched two additional guards to escort the screaming princess back to her room, but they alone couldn't perform the task. Adrina grabbed a door jamb and began kicking. It took four guards to drag her away. Isador watched in approval. It was for Adrina's own good, and her escorts were very gentle despite her verbal and physical abuse.

She threatened to have them all hung; they insisted they only acted on orders. Isador attempted to calm Adrina down as she strode behind the guards, assuring her that they were only performing their duty. After Adrina was locked in her room, she apologized for berating them; still they wouldn't allow her free passage though they were greatly relieved to hear her expression of regret. Even though they had acted on orders, they did fear her wrath. Two of the guards remained outside Adrina's door and the other two hurried back to get further orders from their sergeant.

Father Francis and Chancellor Yi were rushing down the hall when the two guards found them. "It is urgent, Father, you must come quickly!" shouted one of them.

"What is more important than meeting Sister Midori and her party?" snapped Chancellor Yi. He had been so wrought up lately, he had just responded without thinking. "Where?"

"Second Captain Der is conducting a search of the western wing!" said the guard running back down the hall.

"Yes, yes, I know. But have they found anything?"

The guard didn't respond, and the chancellor was forced to chase after him with Father Francis following at a more moderate pace. At a crossing of corridors, they chanced upon Captain Brodst, who was just returning from the search. The chancellor and the captain called out to each other almost at the same moment. Yi spoke hurriedly, for time was short. He winced as he pictured Midori chastising the poor watchmen; for he knew that no matter what she said, they would not allow her entrance to the palace, especially after he had made an example out of the unfortunate lad who had let the nanny Isador pass his post.

"We have searched the whole of the western wing. We did not find anything. I am sorry." The captain told a partial truth.

"No reason to be sorry, good captain," Yi spoke quickly, "go on to the old section in the lower wing and then on to the eastern wing."

"Yes, chancellor," said the captain, also in a hurry to return to his search.

He didn't believe the report one of the guardsmen had given him, and he was determined not to pass an unfounded rumor on to the chancellor. Yi had too many other concerns to worry about. He would search out the truth in the rumor if there were one to be found.

Chancellor Yi commended Captain Brodst and the guards present. He also apologized again for having to make a hasty departure. He didn't want the captain or the watchmen to get the impression that he was uncaring. He and Father Francis hastily dashed off. Although he had received word that Midori had entered the city, he hoped by some charitable twist of fortune that her entourage had been delayed in the city streets. As he entered the main courtyard, however, he knew she had not been delayed. Even from a distance, he could hear her belligerent scream. Again he winced and again he pitied the guards who were enduring her fury. He was winded from his long walk through the palace and walked at the fastest pace he could manage, the slow, stately pace of the statesman.

"I order you to allow me passage to my ancestral home! By right of birth, I am The Princess Delinna Alder, second daughter of King Andrew, king of the entire realm. I will not wait!"

"I am sorry, princess; I have my orders," the guard replied in a terrified whine. Even he knew that she was also a priestess of the Mother and he both feared and revered her.

"From whom, you measly little piss bug?"

"Chancellor Yi himself." The man's voice was only a tiny squeak now.

"Chancellor Yi? I shall have your head if I have to wait one more minute. Do you know what it is to have a sharp edge sever your head from your body? They say that oftentimes you do not die instantly. Did you know that? The Punisher will lift up your severed head so that you may look down at the bloodied stump of your corpse. They say the eyes go wide with mortal shock. To steal a look into the eyes of a dead man is to know what death will be like. Did you know that, you miserable little worm of a man?"

The guard was sweating now, but at least he was on the other side of the gate from her. She could do nothing to him until he allowed her entrance, and he didn't intend to do that.

"I out-rank Chancellor Yi! I order you to let me in now!"

Midori called to the other guard, "You, there! Yes, you! You stupid idiot! Come here!" As he reluctantly approached, Midori yelled, "I order you to arrest this man and let me in! I will even allow you the pleasure of severing his head and grant you life, yet only if you do so at once!"

The guard looked sympathetically to his companion and answered, "I cannot."

"Then you shall both die!"

"Wait a minute, wait a minute!" yelled Chancellor Yi as he approached.

He gestured to the guards to lift the gate. Neither moved.

"Do so quickly, you miserable slugs!" hissed Midori.

Still, neither man moved.

"Now, now, calm down. No one is going to be killed here this day, I promise you," reassured the chancellor.

The guards looked at one another, still unwilling to move. Midori raised her hands and snarled at them again.

"You don't even have them properly trained!" she scoffed.

Chancellor Yi patted the nearest watchman on the shoulder.

"It is all right. I assure you no harm will befall you."

Midori snickered. She was enjoying the show, as were the others in her party.

"I have a wife and two of the cutest little boys you ever did see," quietly spoke the man, nearly in tears.

The other guard nodded.

"You can rest easy. You have my word," whispered the chancellor in as gentle a tone as he could manage.

The gate was eventually raised, but both men kept a good distance between themselves and Midori. As the chancellor ushered her party in, Midori whirled around and lunged at the first man. She stopped, touching her outstretched index finger to his throat. The man nearly swallowed his tongue as he gulped for air.

"Now, now," chastised the chancellor, "there is no need for further harassment."

Midori laughed and walked on. Anger held to her features even as she stepped into the palace entry-room. When Yi ordered her entire party searched before he let them proceed, the face that had only shown anger became enraged. Father Francis assured her that it must be done.

She listened only because she respected this priest of the Father, yet she still thought the chancellor was an old toad. The chancellor handled the entire situation with diplomacy, and by the time the page arrived to show Midori and her two companions to their temporary quarters, she was calmed down.

Yi also sent several guards with them to escort them and remain with them to protect and watch over them. He specifically ordered them to be conscious of the movements of the guests within the palace. He told Midori that he would return later after they had settled in and bathed. After returning to his study he asked Father Francis to find Adrina. Midori didn't like the idea of her escorts, but she didn't make any further comments to Chancellor Yi. She knew the palace well enough to give any guard the slip if need be.

She remained quiet the entire way until the door was closed and then she screamed furiously.

"Catrin, this is an insult to me and to the priestesses. I am not to be treated that way. My Father shall hear about this!"

"Sister Midori-shi of the Eternal Flower, it will all be rectified once we talk to King Andrew," assured Catrin.

Midori fixed her with an angry glare. She hated being addressed with her formal name of office. Sister Catrin reminded her that she was only the fourth to the Mother. She also subtly reminded her that she, Catrin, held higher office and should be the one who was upset.

The priestesses of the Mother were a very secretive group; seldom did they interfere with the ways of the world. They represented the hands of the Great-Mother, silently carrying out her will. The Mother was also the protector of the children of the Father, and so now they must act.

Jasmine looked at the two sisters and smiled knowingly. The two were always bickering, yet only Sister Catrin knew how to end any further conversation instantly. She simply struck Midori where it hurt the most, her pride. When she first came to the priestesses, Princess Delinna Alder had been something. She was a princess of the kingdom; but once she accepted the role of servitude, she became nothing. She had to re-earn a title, a place with the Mother, a difficult thing for a feisty, arrogant girl to do.

Now she was the fourth to the Mother; Catrin was the third. Catrin and Midori had both come to them as girls, not even women yet. Time had been good to them; they both held high offices although Catrin was always one step ahead of Midori. Jasmine knew the reason: Midori's pride was her downfall. She had great potential, and Jasmine hoped one day Midori would take her place as first priestess. Yet this day was a long way off.

After they had relaxed sufficiently, Midori called for the page and the three went to bathe. When they returned, a stranger waited for them. It took Midori a mere instant to realize who it was. The last time she had seen Adrina she had been a messy-haired little girl. She ran to embrace her sister. They held each other for a time. Midori's special sense detected a deep disturbance in the trembling figure she held.

"What is it?" she asked.

"It is father."

Midori put a finger to Adrina's lips to silence them. She had sensed it ever since she had entered the palace. She knew without being told that her father had passed. The extra guards around the palace and the closed gates now explained to her how he had died. She did not want to know anything further, yet she did have a question on the tip of her tongue that she wanted to ask but couldn't. Briefly, her eyes went to Jasmine, fixed with vehemence. You knew this, they said. You knew this and you said nothing, they reprimanded. How could you? They appealed.

"I am truly sorry," whispered Jasmine, in a soft, generous voice.

Midori turned back to face her sister, the expectant stare in those eyes drove her to ask what she had not wished to say.

"Did he say anything—of me?" she asked, her voice quivering with the last words.

Adrina attempted to lie and profess otherwise, except that Midori knew her too well. She begged to know what he had said, and if he had mentioned her before he passed. Adrina stopped; she couldn't tell Midori what he had said. She had not told any one exactly what he whispered into her ear yet, not even Yi.

"Go on!" demanded Midori.

"His last words were—" Adrina hesitated and then said, "May the Father and Mother watch over my children—Midori, I can't!"

"I am strong; nothing can hurt me. Go on," demanded Midori.

"Valam my son and my daughters—and my daughters—Calyin and Adrina. And may this kingdom last throughout time by the will of the Mother and the Father. Midori, I am sorry. He meant to—he meant to—but his passing was so quick. He just wasn't thinking clearly."

Midori slumped to the floor. She tried to hold back the deep emotion flowing through her but could not. Catrin and Jasmine made a hasty exit so the two could be alone. Catrin was sorry for what she had told Midori moments before. She could not undo her words; the call of the Father was final. All things must eventually end, be they good or bad, they must end. Midori's long internal torment was also over.

Midori cradled herself on the floor, refusing the comfort of Adrina. She remembered vividly the day she had left Imtal Palace for good, promising never to return. Her memories flowed back to that day, with the visions flooding through her every thought.

"My daughter, it is your duty to marry King Jarom's eldest. It is pre-arranged. It will make for a strong alliance with the Minor Kingdoms. It will be for the good of the kingdom."

"Father I can not. I do not love him."

"Love will come in time; it is learned. Think of others, not yourself."

"Father, I have decided to join the priestesses. You can say that the deal is void, that I have been chosen by the Mother."

"No! The date has already been set."

"But, I love another."

"Who? I'll tear the rogue's heart out. Who is it that has soiled your honor?"

"Please, for me!"

"It cannot be, my child."

"Midori! You will answer me now!" It was Isador who had yelled that.

Isador looked with sadness upon Midori now and then to Adrina. Even with Midori dressed in the flowing gown of a priestess and clutching at her prayer beads, it never ceased to amaze her how much the sisters looked like their mother. Alexandria had had the same long dark hair, the same clear green eyes, the same high-raised cheek bones.

Adrina was wishing she had lied and told her he had forgiven her. Midori would have found out eventually, though, and the pain would have been that much worse. In this way, the pain of the past was also at an end, and perhaps now she could move on with her life and allow past regrets to slip away.

Midori was trembling as she reached out to embrace Isador. Adrina also joined in the embrace. The room was silent as the three wept.

12

A narrow ledge wound its way down into a vast subterranean gorge in the midst of which stood an enormous lake whose emerald waters reflected the off-yellow iridescence cast by the astounding colony of fungi on the ceiling. The dark waters of the mysterious and obviously deep lake lapped at the rocky shore with slow precision, churned methodically by some unseen force. In the center of the lake on an island of unforgiving granite stood the citadel of Ywentir, which resembled a small walled fortress more than a city. A gentle tingling swept over the exposed areas of skin as the group descended into the canyon, and the knowing knew it to be a semblance of the ancient powers, echoing sullenly now, that had constructed and once kept the place.

"How could a place of such power be invaded? An army couldn't get past here, let alone find its way through that maze!" said Vilmos, louder than he expected. The echo carried across the open span. He had meant to think it, yet the words had slipped out.

꧁꧂ In the Service of Dragons ꧁꧂

"Time," was what Noman answered, "time."

They crossed the lake quite easily. A floating platform of stone floating on a pocket of air and magic that ceaselessly and slowly moved back and forth between the shore and the island swiftly accomplished the task. As they approached, the protective gates to the city opened, and they entered without fear. Ywentir was much the same as its former occupants had left it, untouched by dirt or dust. Famished from the day's long trek and the previous night's excursions, finding food became the main objective. They had carried few rations with them, and what little they had brought were already fully depleted. Thankfully the kitchens, which had once serviced thousands, were not far off and were surprisingly well-stocked and amply preserved. There was also an entire pantry totally separate from the kitchens that was filled with dried fish and mushrooms. Concerns over their growing hunger rapidly diminished as a fire was built in one of the great kitchen's smaller hearths.

After they had eaten, Noman pointed out rooms for them. Vilmos retired only after he had checked on Xith several times. His beautiful companion assured him in words that were soft and reassuring that the shaman would be fine come morning. She sat the vigil beside him through the night thinking of another even as she looked down upon him. She had been given a second chance, a chance to correct errors of the past. She would not fail; she would perform in the proper manner and assure her redemption. Briefly, she thought about those she knew to be so far away and how they fared before she came full circle to the present.

The night passed, though slowly. And while there was no indication that daybreak had come at long last, she knew it had.

✳ ✳ ✳

Vilmos greeted the morning with apprehension until he heard a distant grumbling, the sound of Xith's voice, complaining that he didn't need any help and that he was not an invalid. When Vilmos entered the shaman's quarters, all conversation stopped as Xith gawked at him.

"I thought I was hallucinating! Vilmos, it really is you!" and silently Xith added, "Thank you!"

The two embraced for a long time. Xith's heart filled with joy; the sadness of yesterday was gone.

It took concerted effort to get Vilmos to talk about what had transpired from the time he had fallen and the time he had returned. He would not say a word until he and Xith were alone and only then did he speak of what had occurred. He could not remember much except that for a long time he had existed only in blackness. And then in an avalanche of jumbled thoughts he had seen the battle and the fall, and afterwards nothing save the solitary darkness. Vilmos paused when he saw the other walk into the room. He saw the look on Xith's face; her beauty was unmatched by anything he had ever seen.

"I would like to thank you. I owe you—" Xith started to say.

"You owe me nothing," she said softly, coldly.

She hurriedly exited the room, tears of remembrance flowing down her cheeks.

"What did I say?" asked Xith.

"Give her some time, that is all," answered Vilmos. He said nothing more of her and re-started the conversation, explaining how the light, a tremendous, white, searing light had come for him and taken him from the darkness, and how it had faded when she had taken his hand, how warm and soothing her touch had been as she carried him back into the light.

"What is her name?" asked Xith, curiously probing to see how much Vilmos knew about their mysterious savior.

"I don't know. I have asked. She did not say."

"I think you are right," said Xith responding to what Vilmos didn't say. "It is best to leave that question alone. She will tell us if she wants to in time. For now, I will just be grateful."

Xith and Vilmos sat together, quietly thinking, reflecting upon the past and its lessons. Xith was very glad Vilmos had been given another chance, as had he.

Two days and two nights passed without mishap. Ywentir had a peacefulness about it that made it seem apart from the outside world. The occupants dwelled in its sanctioned walls free of cares for a time, time that allowed for the healing of many wounds both physical and mental. While the others congregated in the common area near the great kitchen,

Vilmos and Xith spent most of their time in the shaman's quarters. Vilmos stared into the shaman's eyes, preparing to ask the other for the umpteenth time how he felt. He waited until Xith relaxed back against his feather pillow and then launched the query.

"How are you feeling now?" he asked speculatively.

"Oh, you worry too much; I am fine. Now stop asking me that! Your pretty friend is a mighty healer. I still believe she is a priestess of the Mother."

"No, she is not, I have told you that already."

"I know, I know," chuckled Xith.

Xith still felt as if Vilmos were his son although the friendship between them had seemed to dwindle. Vilmos had barely spoken to him the entire day, and all Xith could do was to recall the boy he had watched grow. Vilmos had gone through many changes recently and he could feel a coldness within the boy who was now a young man. He wished he could explain to Vilmos everything he knew about what had happened to him and what would happen to him in the future, but he could not; there was so much that was taboo to speak of and so much that could change at any moment. He started to ramble into an apology that was cut short.

"Vilmos, I am sorry for—"

"Don't be sorry; it wasn't your fault," said Vilmos.

"Then what is the matter?"

Vilmos screwed up his face as he pulled out the words from his thoughts, "It is just magic. I don't know if I can still use it."

Xith laughed loudly.

"Is that what has been bothering you?"

Vilmos flashed his eyes with honesty, "Yes."

"Of course you can!" said Xith, greatly relieved. That sounded like the Vilmos he had once known.

"It's just that I have tried; the power is there, I can feel it flow through me, yet each time I try to use it, I fail. I can't even set spark for a simple fire!"

Xith was suddenly very happy; he was a teacher once more. Pride surged through him as he explained magic again to Vilmos, starting with how the flow worked, which Vilmos said he understood. They talked for hours, as Xith explained how Vilmos should tap the raw energy, which was where Vilmos was apparently stuck. Xith was sure he blocked the flow with his mind. He needed to release his thoughts and let the energy flow out of him freely. Xith carried him carefully through each step as he had in the beginning, showing him how to divide his thinking, maintain the flow in and out, and maintain concentration.

"Light this," said Xith as he held out a stick in each hand.

"Which?" asked Vilmos.

"Both."

"I can't."

"You won't. Try. You can do it," urged the teacher. "Know you can, and you will."

"But—" objected the would-be neophyte.

"Concentrate. Direct the flow. Clear your mind; think only of the circuit flowing within you, around you, and out of you."

Vilmos tried.

The youngster cried out in glee as he finally set the first spark to the sticks in Xith's outstretched hands. He had finally done it. The block had only been in his mind; the power was still there. He just needed to practice.

Amir entered the chamber and the two, pupil and teacher, grew silent, awaiting his exit. Amir did not remain long; he had just wanted to check on the shaman and see to his wounds, wounds that were miraculously nearly healed. Amir departed with a cordial nod of the head, walking back to the common area where Noman and Ayrian waited. On the way, he passed their new companion. He studied the way she moved back and forth between the hall and her room, not sure where to go. She moves with such grace, he thought. He felt emotions building within himself, emotions he had not had in a very long time.

"May I join you?" the lumbering giant asked in a meek voice.

"Mmmm—sure," she said softly, grinning.

"Why do you so rarely speak, Little One? What troubles you?" asked Amir using the name he had adopted for her.

"It is of no importance."

"I would like to know," he returned in earnest.

"Amir," she said coldly, "I am here for only one purpose, nothing else. I must re-affirm my faith and prove my worthiness. I am here to die." She said it without emotion, as one would say a casual fact.

I am here to die, he repeated in his mind. Amir sensed the pain inside her, and it puzzled and attracted him. He could not comprehend it or her. His beliefs told him one should enjoy what he or she is given, to be happy here on this plane, as well as the next.

"But why? Why must you die?" he bluntly asked.

His kind also had a different understanding of death. One never dies— he or she just passes from one existence to the next. He wondered if she truly meant death. The Little One didn't answer; still Amir perceived something from her that he counted as a response although again it perplexed him.

"I am falling in love with you, my Little One."

"*What?*" she demanded. "Have you heard nothing I have said? Falling in love," she mocked, "falling in love? What are you saying?"

"I have listened, but I do not care."

"What you feel for me is not love, but pity. Do *not* confuse the two and do *not* confuse your feelings. You can NOT love me. I once did love. I can *not* love again," adding to herself in her mind, "only in the end."

Not knowing what to do or say next, Amir looked hurt. He searched for the right words to express his feelings. He had seen tenderness and feelings in her; he had seen it in the way she cared for Xith's injuries. The coldness she pretended was not who she was. He had heard her solemn cries in the night, the soft sobs in her bed when she thought no one else was awake and could hear them. He wanted to reach out and embrace her and chase away the pain with warmth.

"At least let me know your name," he pleaded.

"I am nothing!" she said and ran from him.

Amir yelled after her, "You are something, something very special!"

"Damn it!" he muttered to himself; that had not gone the way he had wanted it to, not at all.

He watched her go. He could see that the feelings inside her were tearing her apart. He would push no further. He sat alone thinking for a long time, deciding finally to join the others for supper. Most had already begun eating by the time he came to the common hall after the slow walk from his chamber; and by the time he arrived, his appetite was lost. Yet he did bite on a small piece of dried fish and a hunk of hard bread, which he managed to finish. He looked up slowly, still abstractedly chewing on the last few bites from his plate as Noman cleared his throat to get everyone's attention and then started to speak.

"We have always relied on the assumption of unity in purpose and on a willingness to be a participant, but no more. Tomorrow marks a day of change, and we can no longer continue on assumptions of loyalty and willingness to act. I would ask each of you, my five companions, even our newest arrival and even my oldest friend, the same question. Do you have the strength, the perseverance, the tenacity, to say, 'I will not give up the struggle once borne, no matter the cost'? Ask yourself this question. The trials that lie ahead are many and will spare no demands upon you."

Purposefully, Noman looked first to the youngest of his companions. Though it was true that he was not rid of the latent powers within him, he was no longer their ward. His rebirth had proved that.

Vilmos considered the question under the weight of the diviner's scrutiny. He nodded affirmatively as a gesture of goodwill and not because of the strong eyes fixed upon his small form.

Noman looked to each of the others in turn and lastly, again with purpose, to the newcomer in their midst, who not surprisingly took the longest to mull over the charge. She considered herself nothing more than chattel. Her role had already been handed to her. She lifted her eyes and nodded yes, for she knew without a doubt that the surprisingly receptive figure before her understood her plight.

"Good, good," spoke Noman in his beneficent way, "but even so, I may ask this question of you once more. Yet for now, let us look to tomorrow."

A playfulness returned to his eyes. "Then we shall prepare to leave tomorrow. Xith is regaining his strength rapidly, so I think it best we leave as soon as possible."

"Where to?" blurted Vilmos, "Where are we going?"

Xith smiled. This was the Vilmos he knew, always asking questions. "We shall journey towards the sea, I think. Am I correct, Master Noman?" he asked with a wink directed to the guardian.

"Yes, but we will have to cut through the Barrens to do so," offered Noman to give the youngster something more to mull over.

The Barrens, Vilmos remembered, were a vast dry land southwest of the great northern range. He had never been through the desert; it didn't sound like a good place to journey through. Sand and heat didn't excite his sense of adventure, especially if the rugged border country was an indicator of what he could expect from it. He had had enough of dust and wind.

Noman smiled at the eager youth and while the others started to converse freely amongst themselves, he stole the opportunity to confer privately with Xith. He continued to see only partial shadings of the paths ahead and what little he was able to glean troubled him—the shades of darkness spread across the lands and they would have to hurry if they were to gather the last of the lost in time. As he talked with the shaman, Noman continued this inward search, curious now that he saw two faces clearly when before he had only seen the one, that of the girl.

The direct path east to the sea suddenly seemed an improbable route—this was the issue of ever-present change. He told no one of this, not even the shaman, with whom he shared many of his secrets. He and Xith were much alike, he the guardian, and he the watcher. Their conversation soon turned to idle chatter and after a short while they rejoined the others.

When everyone except Vilmos and Xith had retired, the two started into a deep conversation. Vilmos' thoughts at supper had returned to magic. A part of him felt somehow cheated; he had held the power, so great, in his hands, and now it was lost to him. He wanted to learn stronger incantations than the few simple ones he could invoke and the strongest sort of magic he could think of was teleportation, which he wondered if the shaman would ever teach him.

Xith strained to get the point across. True teleportation was a very difficult feat. But Vilmos still wanted to know how it was done. Xith was able to steer the conversation in different directions for a time, but he was never quite able to totally avoid the subject.

"I will teach you in time—patience, Vilmos," admonished Xith.

"What is wrong with now?"

"You will need all your strength for tomorrow…"

The eyes eager for information drove words to the shaman's tongue. "Youth," mumbled the shaman to himself as he considered the hungry eyes.

"Okay, yet I won't teach you that. I'll teach you this!" said Xith, his eyes lighting up as he set his mind to the task of the flow.

The small-statured shaman suddenly loomed larger than life before Vilmos. He lurched forward, his hands stretched far apart. Tiny crackles, sparks of energy, sprang between his fingertips and it was these tiny flicks of energy that lit the shaman's face, cast odd shadows behind him, and made him seem closer than he actually was.

There was a sparkle captivated in the dark pupils of the forthright eyes that happily mirrored the play of the shaman's hands. The unobtrusive sparkle grew in intensity until it became a bolt of solid energy that flowed from one hand to the next, almost enveloping the fingers. The air was crisp with the crackling sound of thunder and Vilmos' hair sparked with static electricity. The bolt grew to a brilliant, deep blue, changing in a surge to a light sky blue.

"This is something you will find extremely useful," said the shaman with a grin, "this is positive energy."

The light shimmered and faded to a faint, white-yellow hue, casting an eerie glow about the room, and the eyes no longer reflected the color with glee; rather, they glittered dully and in a way that was somewhat glum. Vilmos watched intensely, fascinated, captivated.

"This is negative energy…

"At the base of all forces, there are two forms of energy, positive and negative, and they exist in all things. You and I are creatures that fall into the shadow of the realms of the positive. There are creatures, as you have witnessed, that fall into the realms in opposition with our own; they hold the negative."

The shaman inched closer as he spoke, his lips were now only mere inches away from Vilmos' own. The young man's eyes were wide.

"It is possible to harm a creature of positive energy with a form of positive energy, but another form of positive energy could cause the creature to grow." Xith flashed his eyes. "In strength, in size, in abilities. You must choose the form you will use with great care and in time you will learn which type of energy works best for you. Remember that all things stem from these two basic forms. Fire, earth, water and air are reflections of these two forms."

Xith flashed his eyes again.

"A red hot fire will burn you *yes*, but a cool yellow flame will sting you just the same." Xith stopped for a moment, and quite pleased with himself for having conceived the truism, he paused a moment longer.

"Once you choose, you may learn the various forms of that energy and use them to your advantage. I prefer the positive; it is the way my thinking is oriented. It is hard for me to reverse the flow of my energies to form the negative energy. A gifted few are able to use both with equal skill, a very difficult feat. For now you shall practice with them both."

Vilmos sat lost in deliberate thought; something inside his mind clicked. He understood what positive and negative was.

"They are what you used on the trolls; what I used on them."

"Yes, in a way that is true. You were a different person then. Can you remember how you did it?"

"It seemed to flow into me. I could not control it."

"Let us go through the steps of gathering and focusing once more. Listen with your ears, but open your mind and follow with your thoughts." Xith took a deep breath and began in a singsong tone that drew the young man in and made him want to listen. "Gather the energy into yourself. Store it. Clear your mind, cleanse away all outer thoughts. Close your eyes. Concentrate. Release the energy out one side of yourself through your hands; bring it in through the other side. Feel the flow of renewal."

Vilmos practiced.

Xith was pleased at the relative ease with which the pupil found the source of his power.

"That is positive energy. Now, simply reverse the flow through yourself. Be very careful never to mix positive and negative energy, for when the two forces meet unabated they cancel each other out, and you, my friend, will be dead in an instant!" Xith snapped his fingers for emphasis. "Using negative energy is more difficult and requires greater concentration. You must completely re-orient your thinking."

It was morning when the two finished, yet neither showed any signs of tiring from the long night's activities.

Noman just shook his head when he discovered the two still sitting and talking in the same spot they had been in when he had last seen them.

All had a light breakfast and then as much supplies as they could carry were packed. When all was ready, they departed through the maze of Ywentir, finding themselves outside in a short time in the bright sunshine of a beautiful, fresh day and beneath a sun that at high day filtered down into the very floor of the canyon, chasing even the last of the lingering shadows away.

13

Returning as he had promised, Chancellor Yi paused outside the chamber door. Jasmine and Sister Catrin waited in the hall. They indicated that he should not go in, so he told them he would return at a more appropriate time and hastened away. He was already in the outskirts of the lower wing, and he continued on to seek out those who had conducted the search. He was not pleased with the news that they had still found nothing. He ordered the search halted until later that evening. There was much to prepare for Princess Calyin's arrival.

Seated in his small official chamber, Yi got through the day as best as he could. The surface of his desk was buried under an avalanche of partially written scrolls and discarded proclamations; and he looked down at them, no quill in hand now, with indifference. He couldn't find the eloquent words that eluded him no matter how hard he sought them. He wasn't even angered as the door sprang open without a proper knock. He was too tired to find emotion.

"Chancellor Yi, Keeper Q'yer has returned," announced the page.

"Show him in at once," said the chancellor.

"Ahh, Keeper Q'yer, do you have word from South Province?"

The old man's eyes perked up and a touch of color returned to his cheeks as he spoke.

"Yes, chancellor, but I am afraid it is not good news. I received a dream message last night. The council convened this morning, and when it was over I came directly here."

Chancellor Yi sat, expectantly waiting for Q'yer to explain and when he didn't he asked, seemingly exasperated, "Well?"

"They may have already departed. Oh, it is so damned unclear."

"Keeper Q'yer?" asked Yi, in a shocked tone. He had never heard the keeper swear. "Are you all right?"

"Yes, yes, of course I am. It is just so frustrating, that is all."

The chancellor was relieved to hear that someone other than him was frustrated and confused. A Lore Keeper shouldn't be so flustered. Yi allowed the notion to pass, thinking that perhaps it was the burden of the other's newly appointed office.

"Can you contact Keeper Martin?"

"We have tried and are unsure if he received the message. We will keep trying. I bring other news as well. The council is troubled. We have lost contact with the keepers in the minor kingdoms, all contact— and, and—

"The delegates we sent were never heard from again after our earlier council with the nobles. What of Calyin? Has the princess arrived?"

"Midori has already arrived. Once Princess Calyin arrives I plan to make the proclamation of death. If I can ever get the words in order."

"Has the culprit been found yet?"

"No, and it does not bode well. For now the search has been halted, at least until this evening."

"The funeral will still be delayed as we discussed, until all that is at hand is apparent. Correct? That way all those who wish to pay their respects may come and we may have time to deliberate."

"Yes, yes," muttered the chancellor.

"Do you wish the council to state the declaration tomorrow?"

"No. Please have them do it today."

"What of Calyin?"

"She should be here prior to nightfall. Proceed today with the setting of the sun. It was always King Andrew's favorite time. The mourning period is to start immediately afterward."

"I will stay and give it personally. Then I will return to the council. Perhaps I can help you with that speech."

"You are a good man and a good friend. This desk is a mess, is it not?"

The keeper grinned and the two set about putting the proper words to paper. Many minutes slowly crept by, turning languidly into many hours.

∞∞ In the Service of Dragons ∞∞

Princess Calyin and Lord Serant arrived late in the afternoon without incidence. Chancellor Yi stood waiting for their entourage at the palace gates. At least, thought Yi, he was well prepared for their arrival, and he was also on time. He hoped everything would keep moving in a positive direction. The princess' entourage stretched long through the city streets. A crowd was gathering to witness her homecoming. No such crowd had gathered for the other princess' arrival.

Although extremely travel weary, Princess Calyin's escorts held their heads high as they paraded through the capital. Chancellor Yi, who delivered an official welcome, greeted them warmly. It was a grand occasion, to be followed by an announcement of great sorrow. Once the greetings were over, Yi quickly and tactfully set about giving the bad news to the princess and her husband, and then the announcement went out to the people.

Calyin was very calm during the proclamation. She held her head regally high until she reached the safety of the closed doors of her quarters, where she wept openly. Lord Serant held her tightly and comforted her. He understood her pain; his parents had both been killed when he was a child. He knew what it was like to feel loss; he sincerely hoped she did not feel alone with him next to her.

A knock on the door caused Calyin to start, even though she had been expecting it. Both Adrina and Midori had come to greet and console her. More or less, they all comforted each other. They each had loved their father very deeply. Since their mother was already gone, they had thought that he was all they had left, but they were wrong; they had each other.

Lord Serant decided it was best to leave them alone for a time. He went in search of Chancellor Yi. He was angry, and his mind screamed out at the outrage he felt. He would have the man's head if his negligence were to blame for Andrew's death. Two of his personal guards followed him as he charged down the hall. The lord didn't need to look to know that they were there, nor did he need to insure that others still watched Calyin's door. They were his most trusted servants and wordlessly followed his unspoken orders. He paused, listening at the chamber door. A faint woman's voice came into the hall.

"—Chancellor Yi, so you see why Adrina must accompany us—"

Jasmine's sentence was cut short as Lord Serant burst into the room unannounced.

"You vile creature, leave my sight!" shouted Lord Serant as he saw the priestess in the room. He tolerated Midori because she was family, but this one was not. Jasmine taunted him with sweeping motions in the air, but when Serant reached for his sword, she immediately and swiftly left the room. She well knew his scorn for her kind—all those of the territories held hatred for her kind.

"You would do well to forget what you have learned," retorted Jasmine, a last thrust at bravery.

"You would do well to hold your wretched tongue!"

Serant's bodyguards quickly closed the door as Jasmine exited. Fear was evident in their eyes as they did so; they were very careful not to get too close to her. Lord Serant's frown turned to a smile as he greeted Chancellor Yi. He was careful not to say too much, for he wanted to judge the man's undisturbed reaction. He wanted to know if the chancellor were in any way guilty or an accomplice to the dark deed. His sense of perception was very highly tuned and he relied heavily on it. It had to be; otherwise he would not be a former Lord of the Western Territories. High Province was his home now, but his roots were forever in the territories. He still made the pilgrimage to Zashchita and Krepost' once a year. It was his ritual of remembrance.

"You did not have to chase her out," said Chancellor Yi, "Jasmine is a very warm person once you get to know her."

"I am sure you would think so," replied Lord Serant.

Serant eyed Chancellor Yi, checking his expression to note whether he should cut the man's heart out for the insult he had just been given or not.

The chancellor was quick to add, "Your lordship, of course. I have forgotten my manners"; but in his mind he thought, what a backwards people.

"Do not tempt me again. I will not hesitate a second time to perform my right."

Chancellor Yi swallowed hard. He knew what privilege the lord spoke of.

"What is it that your lordship seeks?" he replied cordially.

After his apology, the conversation still continued at a sluggish pace, which extremely agitated Chancellor Yi. He completely understood Serant's innuendoes; and although he disliked them, he said nothing.

"We were waiting until this evening to finish our searches. Perhaps you would like to lead it?"

"Are you saying you have not even completed the search of the palace grounds yet?"

"You are quick to judge, Lord Serant. Yes, we have searched and searched and searched. We found nothing. I ordered one final search; the western wing is all that remains. Perhaps you would like to come with me. I need to find Father Francis, and then I will get Captain Brodst."

"I know the palace, chancellor. You find Father Francis. I will find the captain."

❊ ❊ ❊

"Father Francis, may we come in?" asked Jasmine.

"Sister Jasmine, I am sorry about before. I should have made formal introductions to Chancellor Yi. Everything is just such a mess right now."

"That is to be expected."

"Why has the first of the Mother ventured from her temple? The message we received said only Midori would return with her aides."

"Sister Midori has returned with her aides," said Jasmine. "We did not intend to deceive. It was just the delicacy of the situation. Many considerations had to be taken into account. I am here for a very important purpose. We two follow parallel paths do we not?"

"Similar yes, parallel no," rebuked the priest.

"No need to be harsh. I was merely suggesting. The Mother has spoken to me. I must take Princess Adrina away. It is for her own protection."

"I see shadings of another reason, a selfish reason."

"You accuse me of—" Jasmine was growing angry.

"Yes, most certainly! I know your ways. What would you do with the child?"

"Care for it, of course," spoke the priestess slyly.

"And raise it according to your ways. I speak for the Great-Father and also, I believe, for the Mother-Earth. The child's destiny lies not with you. Adrina will remain here! Did you think that since King Andrew is dead you could just come here and take Adrina away?"

"I did not know the old buffoon was dead. We just chanced on an opportune time."

"Buffoon? Get out of my sight! Go, before I have you thrown out!" screamed Francis, "If you were not with Midori, I would have you flogged for heresy!"

"Publicly or privately?" mocked Jasmine.

"*Get out*!" ordered Francis.

Jasmine nearly knocked Yi down as she vaulted into the corridor.

"My word!" gasped the chancellor.

"My word indeed, you old crow! You'll all get what you deserve!" shouted the priestess as she and Catrin retreated.

"What was all that for?" asked Yi, as he stepped into the priest's room.

"A slight disagreement, nothing more," replied Francis.

A guardsmen approached from the hall. "Chancellor Yi, Chancellor Yi!" shouted the guardsman, "Come quickly! Captain Brodst has been looking for you."

"Tell the good captain he can wait a moment. I was just on my way to see him… Go along now, boy."

"But, Chancellor Yi, you do not understand. You have to come and see. They think they have found the assassin." The young guard was so excited that he spoke frantically and too quickly to be understood.

"Don't use that word, boy. Now slow down and say that again."

The words were repeated.

"Where?" was all Yi said.

"The eastern wing. Come, I'll show you."

ॐ In the Service of Dragons ॐ

The two old men were not as quick on their feet as the lad, and the other had to pause continually so they could catch up. He led them down several corridors, twisting this way and that, through a small open courtyard into the opposing wing, up two staircases and down a last lengthy hall. A large clump of guards filling the hallway moved so the two could pass. Yi recognized the room they were guarding; it was Father Jacob's room. The door was ajar and sounds of a commotion could be heard.

One of the guards, a sergeant, darted inside and retrieved Captain Brodst. The captain did not have a pleased expression on his face.

"Chancellor, you had better wait out here."

"Have you found him?" asked the chancellor.

"We have found something, that is certain. Please stay here until this is settled."

The captain was suitably gruff and terse. He waited in the hall no longer than he had to. Chancellor Yi didn't have to be told not to follow; as the door swung open and then shut, he saw several dead bodies littering the floor. He knew the danger. Father Francis followed the captain into the room and closed the door behind himself, intent on saying the last rites. He wasn't prepared for what he found. Three guards lay dead on the floor, another lay wounded near death, and still two others battled with a creature in the corner of the room.

"It appears trapped!" yelled 2nd Captain Der as he and several others battled the creature.

Father Francis was a man knowledgeable in the lore. He recognized the trapped creature. A quick scan of the chamber revealed to him why the thing had been drawn to the room and trapped within. He thought to himself that Father Jacob was a smart man. A shadow, whispered the priest to himself, suddenly reminded of the child's tale concerning such a creature. Speak its name and it shall disappear, he said, again in a whisper, adding power to the words of the tale.

"Shadow be gone," he intoned in a light voice that didn't even rise above the cacophony of shrieks and shouts.

The child's tale proved to be only that, a child's tale.

"You are lucky that it is so weak now!" yelled Francis, raising his voice above the howling cackle the creature was starting to make.

"Lucky?" yelled Captain Brodst looking to the dead.

Captain Der shouted, "Should I finish it?"

The shadow was beginning to fade with each consecutive blow.

"Yes!" screamed Francis, whispering, "If you can." He added, after a moment of thought, "We will get no information from this being!"

The shadow and Father Francis locked eyes as he spoke. It waited until Francis stopped talking and then as it cackled wildly, it lunged, sweeping past the captain, straight for Francis. It had heard his barely audible whisper and it mocked him with its attack. His soul, the soul of a holy man, would bring greater reward than the souls of the three it had already devoured. Its icy fingers clasped the priest's throat, ripping at it as the two fell to the floor.

Another guard jumped into the fray, followed by Captain Brodst, who until now had been watching the creature, studying it. The guard hacked at the shadow. Captain Der blocked the blow with his sword and cuffed the guard with his elbow and then in the face with the back of his free hand. All the guards backed away from his wild grin, fearing his blade and thinking him mad. They waited, vying for the opportunity to tackle him.

Captain Brodst stood steady, unmoving. He watched the others and the second captain. He threw his hand up in a signal of halt, just as the others were about to pounce. Hold off, he beckoned. Watch, wait and pray, he indicated.

The shadow howled in glee, squeezing its icy, clawed hands tighter around the priest's throat. Only the aura of good the All-Father granted the priest saved him and allowed him a few more frantic moments of survival. Father Francis struggled against the weakened will of the creature. Good and evil clashed. He cursed its darkness with the name of the Great-Father, seeking to send it back to where it had come from. The raven-hued shadow shimmered with a silver light, revealing its true form. Father Francis cursed the darkness and again cleansed himself in the name of the Father, bathing in the might of good. A high-pitched squeal emitted from the shadow as the silver light intensified, gathering not only along the outer edge but also bursting up from within the center of the black form, tiny eruptions of good. With a final shriek, the shadow winked out of existence.

Father Francis chased after the shadow with his own mocking form of prose. "There is truth to be found in children's tales. You have only to believe," he whispered.

Captain Der helped the priest to his feet. The other guardsmen moved to engage the captain, still fearing him mad. Father Francis was quick to calm them. He turned to the perplexed guard and said, "If your blow was not blocked, I would not be here now. They are unlike us. They are a form of energy. They can shift their substance. Your blow would have gone through it into me. Second Captain Der knew this, and in his own way, he was protecting me."

"I am sorry Father Francis, I thought—"

"It is a natural mistake, there is no need for an apology. Come; let us be gone from this room! There is a foulness in the air."

Chancellor Yi heard the fighting stop and entered the chamber with two guards in front of him.

"Father Francis, what has happened? Are you all right?"

"We have found your assassin!"

"You have?" he said as he looked about the room, seeing only the dead guards.

"It was a shadow, a dark assassin; that is why we could not find it. A twist of fate and luck carried it to this room and once here it was trapped."

"But how?" asked Yi not quite understanding, not really thinking either.

"This is Father Jacob's room correct?"

"Yes, yes it is—"

"See the signs on the walls. Those are wards to keep away evil. Unfortunately, yet fortunate for us, if evil somehow finds it way inside them it is trapped."

"Who would have sent it and how would it have come to Imtal Palace?"

"How and who indeed, my friend. We shall have to wait and see. Let us hope we will have no more such visitations. I don't think I could handle the strain again. Such a test of faith."

Father Francis crossed himself and said a silent prayer.

"Praise be to the Father," he whispered.

14

The small band walked through the narrow canyon at a moderate pace, the bleak stone walls seeming a hollow prison, and Vilmos felt trapped within them. He couldn't wait for the burst of greenery that he hoped lay somewhere ahead, the place where the dead-black prison ended and life began. He neglected to recall that beyond the canyon west and east lay mountains and a long series of rolling foothills.

He had been told that one path would bring them to the mountains, another would carry them into the foothills and beyond to the Borderlands, and yet another would carry them to the distant wastelands of the Barrens. The sun was no longer directly above, so now numerous shadows lurked not far off. Vilmos looked out at this world of shadow and light as if he saw through a layer of dense fog. His thoughts were unclear and old memories streamed into his mind as he looked about, memories that were not his own, but the others'. The air was cooler than he remembered it.

Behind him, Amir and Noman were deep in conversation and although he couldn't fully hear what they discussed, he could guess. The two had been talking about the same topic since they had begun, the subject of which was beyond his comprehension. Looking to the front and again to the rear, Vilmos regarded the little flock. Everyone was present except for Ayrian, whom he had not seen since the outset. He wondered where he was.

Vilmos carried on, his gaze from time to time returning to the diviner and the warrior. He looked back to the others also, Xith and the Little One. Every now and again, little lines of sunshine played upon her face in a myriad of patterns and every now and again she would flick the thick tuft of hair that would fall down over her eyes back into place, always blowing it up with a puff of air at first and then raising frustrated hands to toss it back when that didn't work.

The shaman walked with the aid of a twisted oaken stave, which he had retrieved along with many other trinkets from amongst his belongings stored at the hidden city. A clear blue ball was fixed into the crown of the twisted dark wood, set within the grasp of an upturned clawed hand. The tapping of the stick against the rocky trail created a resonant sound that echoed boldly from the canyon walls, which didn't seem to bother the shaman in the least though it irked Vilmos.

Not looking where he was going, Vilmos stumbled and nearly fell. It was only Amir's fast hand that saved him from a nasty spill. He brought his attention back to his surroundings. The trail had grown suddenly rockstrewn and he needed to pick his way through it with care. For a short while, he kept his attention on the trail, picking up one foot and placing it down and then picking up the other and setting it down without faltering. His mind was at ease as this occupied the moments he had been squandering in distress.

The path eventually cleared and Vilmos raced to catch up with the others, surprised to find that they had reached the end of the canyon. He cast no glances behind as he sprang along down the long decline that he hoped would lead out of the gorge. He looked forward to the sight of rolling hills spreading out before him and perhaps even patches of thick green grasses. He scrambled on, stopping abruptly as the illusion of the facing wall disappeared. The wall was an illusion from afar, for the narrow canyon split into two gorges that were narrower still. Puzzled, for he hadn't noticed this the first time through; he scratched his head absently.

The pace quickened now as deep shadows began to gather around them. The day was nearly spent. Xith urged them on, saying that he wanted to be in and out of the tunnels before nightfall. Vilmos' heart nearly skipped a full beat at the mention of tunnels. He didn't look forward to traipsing through any more dark tunnels under any circumstances, let alone when his nerves were already unsettled by the arrival of darkness.

"The tunnels will take us through the mountains—that is, if I can find them and find the way through them. It has been quite some time," said the shaman, "and with any luck, we'll be in and out before you know it."

They found the entrance to the tunnels some hours later, but it did not seem that luck was on the travelers' side. The shadows in the gorge were already deep and full, and night was perhaps only a few hours away.

"Stay close," warned the shaman, as he led the way.

Here the order changed; Noman came up beside Xith and Amir took up the rear. Vilmos and the Little One were ushered into the more protective middle ranks.

Xith didn't sound very reassuring when he told them that hundreds of tunnels ran through the mountains, yet only one or two came out directly. "The others could lead us around for days. Not to worry, though; I am sure that this is the one we want to follow."

The hills seemed so desperately far away.

"Stand ready to move fast if need be. Some areas are pretty unstable and the supports may be worn through. You can rest easy, though, because I don't think any manner of beast would take up residence in this section of the tunnels unless of course—well, never you mind." The shaman's voice trailed off as the small band passed into the shadows of the rock.

Noman lit their way with a magical flame. The blue flame was familiar and somehow, in the later hours, became a thing that reflected relative safety to their minds. Perhaps it was the soothing blue-white color or perhaps just the fact that it showed the way through the darkness. Goosebumps faded from unsettled skin and the dankness and the cold became no longer hindrances.

Oddly enough in the new subterranean world that was revealed, even amongst the dampness, the darkness, and the cold, there were things of beauty to behold. A few of the great cavernous rooms they came across held natural wonders, intricate series of stalactites and stalagmites spread out in a myriad of shapes and sizes, all yearning to reach one another. One particularly grand grotto held a large, perfectly circular pool filled with seemingly clear waters with a great stalagmite in its center. Vilmos nearly wandered over to the pool, but Xith quickly snatched him away from it.

The sense of the flow of time, the ticking away of minutes and hours, became difficult to discern. For some it was an endless wait, filled with hours upon hours of yearning to see a burst of color or light that would mark their exit from the darkness, yet for others it seemed that time held no consequence for them.

Xith trudged on with sure feet despite some grumblings.

A light meal was eventually taken in a small cavern that they had stumbled across. The ten-foot square cavelet held but one entrance and seemed safe enough, so packs were dropped and food stores were delved into. It was midway through the meal when Xith noticed the wardings marked on one of the walls. They had been etched by his own hand on a trip a long time ago. He started, dropping his meal to the ground, and stood and walked over to the wall, his face masked in a deep, dark frown.

"Oh my," he gasped, and by then all eyes were upon him.

"What is it, shaman?" asked Noman.

There was a faraway look in the other's eyes as he turned back to face them and began. "You—wouldn't—believe—even—if—told you—"

"I would," whispered the Little One, to the surprise of the others.

"It was here that it happened—almost a lifetime ago," whispered the shaman in a voice almost unfamiliar to the others. Perhaps it was the sorrow held in the tone, or other things, but it seemed the voice of a different man than the one who stood before them.

Xith fell to his knees as he ran to a dark splotch on the floor, running his hand over the wide, dark blemish. "Right here is where he fell. He was in so much pain."

Xith straightened his hunched-over back and rubbed tears from his cheeks. "I didn't know why we ran towards instead of away, not until that moment, that very sad moment. It is not a pleasant thing to hear the gasps of the dying, so much pain, so great a struggle to tell all that needed to be said—to find that you alone carry on the struggle."

"You are not alone, Shaman of the Great Northern Reaches, nor were you ever truly alone." It was Noman's voice that surprisingly sprang forth, "for if you had been, none of us would be here now with you.

Ywentir may have fallen, but there were those of us who held Tsitadel', and those that survived were given a second chance."

"Yes, but they came for us and hunted us down like animals."

"Yet your father and mother survived and were blessed with a son, passing down their life memories to you so that you carried them on."

The downcast eyes straightened and the strong emotions cleared. "We took a wrong turn back there. We need to retrace our path a short distance and then—"

"No, the sun set long ago. I think it best if we remain here," spoke Noman with finality. "There is a sense of goodness in this small place. We can rest easy; no harm will befall us, of this I am sure. It is sometimes a healing experience to relive the pain of the past."

✳ ✳ ✳

Low hills spread out ahead in a long, seemingly endless series of hunchbacked rises. It almost seemed as if the travelers could simply step across them without having to descend into the veiled falls, but they would soon discover that progress through the hill country was not as easy as it seemed. The companions raced on, eager to make up the few hours of lost time.

As he walked the course, Vilmos vaguely remembered having passed through the low hills before. He watched the shaman continually cast sidelong glances up into the cloudless blue sky and often into the distance far ahead, without knowing what the other watched for. The hills were not entirely bleak and lifeless as he knew the lands that lurked ahead would be. He saw small rodents scurrying about their daily chore of gathering food and even small birds nested in the branches of the scrub trees waiting for the opportune meal to present itself.

Afternoon was settling upon the travelers now; they would have to hurry if they wanted to be out of the hills by nightfall. Vilmos breathed deeply and easily now as he finally realized no more shadows surrounded them. Momentarily, he hesitated and looked back; over his left shoulder lay the mountains, which seemed to lurch suddenly into place only as he looked back.

Over his right shoulder there was an empty patch of brown and tan that faded away to gray; and while he couldn't see the mountains that he knew should be there, he could guess that they were, in fact, there somewhere. Ahead, he still saw only the hills, even as he topped a new rise. The sun continued along its westerly path and the travelers continued south, trudging along; and when it seemed the sun was about to dip down to the land, the travelers, at long last, found their way beyond the hills. The group paused here, for here they were supposed to turn east; they stopped to rest and to wait for their companion's return.

The sun had truly dipped beneath the land as Vilmos spotted a single rider ushering a group of horses toward them. An earlier question was answered as the feathered face came into view and Vilmos returned the salutatory wave as did the others.

"I was beginning to think you would not arrive, old friend," called out

Xith.

"I told you I would make it. Two hours of day to spare. Did you not have faith in me?" came the response.

Xith chuckled.

"Yes, I did, yet I was unsure if you would be able to procure the mounts and return in such a short time."

"Swifter than the wind," Ayrian shot back with a quick grin as he dismounted, motioning for everyone to pick an animal and start packing the gear onto it. Time was of the essence.

Amir claimed the largest beast for his own, the only beast that could withstand the burden of his great bulk, an all-white steed with a black nose and two black socks. Still, his enormous size seemed to dwarf that of the horse. Vilmos set his packs upon his chosen animal and hesitantly mounted. He didn't much like the idea of riding, yet it was better than walking. In contrast to the lumbering giant, he had chosen the smallest horse, a brown mare with a long black mane. The others mounted, each in turn, save Ayrian who took no mount. He preferred to return to the air. Vilmos watched the Eagle Lord as they rode away. Golden rays of the sun seemed to dance along the feathered skin, a lush golden bronze and then suddenly Ayrian took flight, launching into the air, his great wings thrashing the earth, sending plumes of dust outward and upward.

The party followed Ayrian as he led them across the long flat basin and, to Vilmos' dismay he led them south instead of east, into another stretch of rugged, low hills. They rode at a fast pace and, as the horses had formerly been riderless, they moved swiftly, allowing the travelers to cover much ground despite the intractable hills. Night did come, though; they could not hold it back no matter how fast they rode, and just within the ring of safety the hill country provided, they set up camp. The weary travelers were quickly asleep and even those who weren't utterly fatigued found sleep swiftly. Dawn came, and with it they stirred. Breakfast was frugal and hurriedly eaten; this day promised to bring rain, and they wanted to put distance between themselves and the encroaching storm. They took a southwesterly path, which would almost immediately take them into the border country. Fear of the storm drove them on and they rode with good speed.

Ruggedness seemed to jump out at Vilmos as the last of the hills leveled out. He remembered the wild magic that had been here, which he no longer felt, and although he did perceive a subtle shift of the energies within him, it was nothing compared to the wildness he had once absorbed. A dry gale kicked up coarse dirt, flinging it into unshielded eyes with a vengeful sting. Kerchiefs were brought up around nose and mouth to the low brim of the eyes. Eastward, the dark tumultuous billows of a storm front approached and Vilmos turned to gawk at it. As he did so, he spotted the Eagle Lord circling loftily overhead.

Vilmos squinted, for suddenly it seemed that Ayrian was no longer there. He rubbed his eyes, thinking something had gotten into his eyes, and then stared again. As he looked on, a thing he at first mistook as an odd cloud, soared past him. For an instant, he recalled his fear of the shadows that the storm was spreading across the eastern landscape, but then recognition came. He roused the stirrups and sent his steed racing to catch up to the shaman. "Xith?" said Vilmos as he rode up beside the other, "How did he do that?"

"Who did what?" asked the shaman, apparently lost in his own concerns.

"Ayrian, look!" he exclaimed and then pointed.

"That is a gift that proved to be the bane of his kind," muttered Xith, "I would suggest you worry about your own concerns. Have you been practicing as I told you to do?"

"Well, no, not really," admitted the apprentice, "can I do that?"

Xith considered Vilmos' words for a time before replying.

"No. It is the Father's gift to his kind. I am afraid he is the last of such shape-shifters in all the land. Through illusion, some may seem to change forms, but they are only real if you believe them. That is a gift you would do best to forget."

Vilmos tugged at the reins to slow the horse a bit.

"But why?" he asked.

"That is a story only Ayrian would tell best. But I will tell you some. After all, we have a long ride ahead of us. Do we not?"

Vilmos signaled agreement with a hearty nod.

In spite of the wind, the dust, and the clatter of hooves against hard ground, Xith began to tell the tale. Vilmos said nothing for a long time as the elder spoke, intent on listening, which alone proved a difficult task. Xith paused and eyed Vilmos to be sure that he still followed; for as the storm approached he was unsure whether the other was able to hear anything he said and then just when he was about to begin again, Noman signaled a timely halt.

"Did you hear anything I said?" asked Xith.

Vilmos shrugged his shoulders. "Not really," he finally admitted. "Do we have time now? I mean to tell it again."

"I'm not so sure that I have the energy to do it," explained the shaman, sighing and then looking to Noman, who winked.

"It is about time for lunch, is it not?" spoke Noman.

Xith nodded and shot a prudent glance at the thunderclouds still looming not far off.

"Do not worry, shaman, they will turn north with the winds and blow up into the mountains. They always do."

Amir seemed to agree as he furrowed his eyebrows and looked at first eastward and then heavenward.

"Five clans once peacefully ruled the whole of the Northern Ranges," Noman began in a winsome tone, beckoning the boy to squat down to his haunches on the hard, windswept ground. "They dwelled happily in the many valleys that dot the range from end to end, for there all their needs were met. The mountains afforded shelter from the elements. The valleys provided food for hunt and meal. They wanted for nothing and infrequently visited their brethren in Over-Earth."

The words echoed resonantly in Vilmos' mind as well as in his ears. The voice that he had thought ranged only in baritone swept from tenor to bass with surprising ease that made it sound natural and to be expected.

"The mountains proved an important barrier, a marshalling wall that spread from the Eastern Sea to the Western Sea. There were other tribes in the Northlands then, too. They dwelled safely beyond the mountains, preferring the bitterness of snow and ice to the concerns of the outside world. My own people often visited and for a time we peacefully intermingled. Yet at this time we had no communities within their lands—that is another tale destined for another telling. We provided the few things that the Eagle Clans had found they lacked. And it was through our comings and goings that Man discovered the Eagle Clans.

"The spread of Man came as a slow incursion, like a disease festering in an open wound. They had spread south, west and east, until they bordered all their neighbors save one, the peoples of the North. You see, where the others had been given gifts that could not be maligned, Man had been given the gift of Magic.

"Hold that question—I know what you wish to ask already—but then why do the peoples of the Samguinne have magic? And I will tell you that it is because they were its first users. But along with this gift the Father endowed them with understanding and great wisdom. He gave them the power of control and the knowledge of the end that would come if they misused the gift. So in this sense, it was a different gift than he gave to Man. But then you might also ask where does your own gift of magic come from? And I will again tell you that that is another tale for another telling.

"It is not known why Man was not given this same knowledge, and perhaps the Great-Father erred, for surely even with his infinite wisdom he is allowed an occasional error. Perhaps the Great-Father thought that without this knowledge the gift was diluted, but this did not prove so—I digress do I not? Did you not ask Xith about the Eagle Clans, and Ayrian's own gift?"

Noman paused to take a hearty swig from his water bottle and crunch on a bit of dried meat.

"You're not going to stop are you?" asked Vilmos, eager to hear more.

"No, no, but I think it best if you hurried through that bit of meat and bread you hold in your hand, for we cannot sit idle much longer. I must apologize for the brevity I am forced to, but I must try to sum all this up for you in a matter of minutes.

"As I said, there were once five clans, and among them the Gray and the White Clan were the most powerful. It was the White Clan that eventually befriended Man and granted them passage to the North. And ironically it was the White that was the first to fall at the hands of Man.

For you see, Man discovered their gift, the same gift you looked at with awe in your eyes. Not only could the Eagle Clan fly, but they could also grow and be made to carry others. Yet, I get ahead of myself again.

"As Man moved North, the peoples of the Northlands cried out in outrage. The Gray Clan and Ayrian, the Gray Eagle Lord, himself, denounced their brothers and returned to Over-Earth. Now listen, and listen close and remember, for you will find none of what I have told you or none that I am about to tell you in your twisted lore. Man began to enslave those of the White Clan and the White without the aid of their brethren fell easily. Man did not stop there. Magic spells were woven on the hapless prisoners, and they were made to do the bidding of Man. It was Man himself that started the Blood Wars through this treachery. And it was all because of a gift that they could not possess without seizing. On the backs of the White they poured into the North. Settlements were created. Cities grew. Hatred grew."

Noman stopped and drank from his jug again. After chewing on a large piece of jerked meat for a time, he stood. Amir was already mounted though Vilmos did not know this as he had been listening so intently. Noman mounted likewise and Xith followed.

"You're not going to stop, are you?" demanded Vilmos, "I mean, that is surely not the end. Is it?"

"It is," said Noman, gesturing to the youngster to mount up.

"Wait, is there a gift I have?"

"The first sons of the Father were given many gifts, but the Father soon learned that if too many were given, it could lead to destruction. The time of the beginning was such a time; all the wild magic was free. Now it is only there if you are able to attain it. The Father divided different gifts amongst the brother-races. This worked for a time, until those of the beginning returned."

Vilmos mounted as the others prepared to leave.

"Wait," shouted Vilmos, "you didn't answer the question."

"Yes, I did. If you consider the response," returned Noman.

15

Late in the afternoon, the travelers made another stop. Vilmos wanted an opportunity to talk to Noman, but the opportunity failed to come. Afterwards, they continued southward through the Borderlands toward the Krasnyj, stopping only at evenly spaced intervals to rest horse and rider. Ayrian had disappeared across the horizon hours ago; Xith had sent him out to search for a place to camp for the night.

The Borderlands was not a place to be caught unawares. Afternoon had brought a return of the dark patches of shadow that Vilmos dreaded; yet fortunately the storm had veered off northward as Noman had said it would and now only a quiet, dry wind blew across the empty land.

Vilmos also dreaded the thought of a place more desolate than this. How much worse could it be, he wondered. His thoughts slowly returned to concerns over the Eagle Lord's whereabouts. Since they had not seen him for some hours, all were growing concerned, most noticeably Xith, though he wouldn't have admitted it.

And then just when they thought night would come and Ayrian would be absent, he burst into the sky above their heads and landed. Vilmos was the only one who was significantly startled by his appearance although the Little One did appear slightly surprised by it. Ayrian settled quickly and ran over to Xith. The two spoke in hushed tones for a long time; and from the pieces of the conversation Vilmos picked up, he sensed something was awry.

He also began to understand the expression on the Little One's face; she had been less surprised by Ayrian's sudden appearance than by what she perceived from him. Noman and Amir seemed to be off in their own concerns, quietly conversing together, though Vilmos could see Amir checking over his equipment. Amir had unsheathed his great sword, giving the blade an inspection and touching a whetstone to it. Vilmos turned back to the Little One and saw an expression of disbelief on her face. Xith took to saddle; Ayrian borrowed a mount and the two wordlessly rode away. The remainder of the group was to camp here this night and wait until the two returned.

Vilmos felt compelled to say something, any sort of comment would do, though he couldn't decide what. "Are we just going to sit here?" he demanded.

"Patience," advised Amir as he leaned his head back against his pack and closed his eyes.

Sleep came slowly for Vilmos, and just moments after he had closed his weary eyes, he was rudely jerked from his slumber by Xith. The first thing he noted was that the sun wasn't even over the horizon yet, so he rolled over attempting to return to sleep.

"Vilmos!" shouted Xith in his ear.

Instantaneously the youngster was awake, wide-awake. Seeing Xith's long silhouette across the ground, he took a good look at the sky about him for the first time and realized that the sun was still in the process of setting, not rising.

"What is it?" he hissed.

"I'll explain later; for now just get mounted. We can talk later if need be. We must make a detour. Hurry now," said Xith, as he hastened Vilmos to mount.

"Where to?" asked Vilmos.

Xith did not respond.

Noticing that he was the last to stir, Vilmos hastily mounted and spurred the mare several times to urge it into a gallop. They rode the horses hard through that last hour of twilight and long into the night, led on by a faint shadow in the sky. Intermittently, they would dismount and walk, but always they continued to move. Any thoughts of conversation had ended with the darkness of night; now their only concern was to reach their destination, which Vilmos still did not know.

The only thing he was vaguely aware of was that at some point they had veered from the southwesterly path they had begun to a direct southerly route. Only a pale sliver of the moon and the occasional stars were visible in the overcast sky. The darkness gave Vilmos the shivers, and every sound caused him to start. He clutched the sweat-soaked leathers in his hand and hastened the animal on with stronger than usual proddings. They seemed to be in a continual chase or rather as Vilmos perceived it, a continual effort to outrun the dark things that crept up on them from behind.

The land held real shadows now and they truly frightened Vilmos. Intermittently, Xith cursed vehemently under his breath, a sound that carried very well in the empty night air. Vilmos did not question him; they did not have time to spare. The detour would take them a day's ride away from their destination, an extra day that they could not afford to lose. Yet he could not simply ignore what he had seen.

"Damn it!" he cursed again louder as he gnashed his teeth and whipped his steed on.

Daylight came and still they pressed on. Leaving the stale, dead brown of the Borderlands, they entered the green lands of the Kingdom. Unfortunately, they had come too far west in the night and now needed to turn back east—more delay that they could not afford. Vilmos had learned that their destination was Solntse; Xith had told him this in a manner that suggested fear that he might be overheard.

In the light of the new day, Vilmos studied the diversified party he rode with, wondering what the people of the city would think upon seeing their arrival. Ayrian would be their main problem; he was clearly different from them all. Even Amir's immense proportions were nothing compared to the feathers and talons of Ayrian. As he mulled this over, he could feel something, as if eyes were upon him. Another shiver traversed his spine, an ill feeling that even the new day did not diminish.

High noon came and passed, and the riders raced on. They had finally come to the High Road. The legendary East-West Road was still far to the South. That road ran east all the way to Krepost and Zashchita then to the Eastern Seaboard. It was clear and wide and extremely long yet relatively safe. The High Road ran straight east into Solntse and directly west to the Western Sea, cutting a narrow line that formed the unofficial northern boundary of the Great Kingdom.

The High Road was heavily traveled by garrison soldiers, peddlers and rogues alike. Unlike the East-West Road, it was a dangerous though necessary path to follow. The breakneck pace was maintained with all remaining fully alert despite weary bodies and weary steeds. Amir rode to the rear, his eyes continually scanning the countryside and his right hand never leaving the hilt of his great sword. Noman and Xith rode at the fore; Vilmos and the other were in the middle. Ayrian was still somewhere overhead though he attempted to remain unseen for the most part.

The horses were near death and still they raced on; their gallant efforts were not lost to the thankful riders. Beyond a ridge that was only a short distance away lay the Free City, or so Xith promised. Vilmos absently rubbed his weary body and his saddle sores. The journey was nearly complete. The sojourn through the darkness would hopefully prove worthwhile. Even as they climbed the rise that cut off their view of the city, Vilmos braced himself. He knew what lay beyond. But when he at last reached the top of the rise, he still found himself stifling an awed breath. The sight of the city growing in the distance spurred them on, yet as they broke the rise, they were not prepared for what lay in wait for them on its far side.

Noman's mount was the first to be torn from under him, with Xith's soon following. Vilmos only managed to rein his animal to a halt thanks to the swift reactions of the one who rode beside him. She grabbed the reins from his hands even as she jerked her own steed to a halt, pulling them both to a dead stop. It was a desperate, wily group of assailants that set up an ambush this close to the Free City, but even their cleverness and the element of surprise did not prepare them for the inhuman speed of the mighty warrior.

Amir bounded from his saddle, tumbling onto the hard ground, coming up with his sword flashing in his hand like a thing possessed. The would-be assailants never knew what hit them as the first of their ranks fell, one with an upward slice to the unprotected jugular, another with a downward hack through the soft leather armor to the gut.

To his shock, Vilmos watched the man's innards spill into his hands, his face filled with dismay and eyes wide with horror as he staggered and fell flat on his face. Amir didn't stop there; he continued the assault with a lightning speed and a quick precision that only he could have managed, taking so many of the assailants in the first few moments of the brief battle that the survivors were scrambling just to recover from the deadly blows and were on the run before they even had time to counter.

Even as Xith and Noman righted themselves and prepared to return to saddle, the battle was nearing its end. Without thought, Amir dropped the last man, taking him mid-stride in his exposed side as he whirled to run. In a way that was almost casual and made Vilmos' skin crawl, Amir wiped the blood from his blade using the dying man's tunic as the man gasped for his last breath, sheathed the blade, and then without even a backward glance, remounted. There was no exchange of words and the group continued toward the city as if the incident had never occurred.

Several hundred yards from the gates, the group stopped for a quick reprieve and upon Xith's signal dismounted; then and only then did it seem the impact of the incident hit them though still no comments were made. They waited a moment until Ayrian circled down to join them and then walked the horses the remainder of the way to the city. They were stopped at the gates and inspected; after a moment and a small bribe they were allowed entrance.

A stable just within the gates was their first stop and their horses were traded for fresh ones. The stable master charged exorbitant prices for the exchange, yet Xith didn't even argue as he counted off payment to the gray-haired gentleman. He told the owner they would return in the morning and then left to find an inn. They did not immediately explore the city's heart as Vilmos had expected; instead they turned down the first street they came to.

Vilmos walked next to Xith and nudged him. He whispered, "Why isn't everyone looking at us weirdly?"

He had expected their group to draw considerable attention; however, they seemed to go unnoticed. It may have been the simple wish to dispel the somber mood, but the shaman decided to play with the boy and Noman seemed responsive to the notion. Instead of responding directly to the question, he simply pointed to Noman, who already had a smirk on his expressive lips.

Noman told the perplexed young man with a wink, "A simple trick—"

"An illusion," added Xith, mixing a tone of mysticism into his voice as if the presence of a true illusion were not already mystical enough in and of itself.

"They see us as a group of barbarian traders from the border country; that is the reason they made us pay a bribe to get past the gates."

Vilmos looked up, squinting. He didn't see anything. He saw everyone the same as he had before; there was no difference.

Xith whispered to him, "You still see us as we are because you already know who we are, yet someone who doesn't sees us differently."

Vilmos was interested in learning this trick but was disappointed when Noman explained to him that he could not do it. "I'm truly sorry," he said, "It is somewhat of a specialty of mine and I am afraid, try as you might, you will not be able to reproduce it."

"One of his many gifts," added Xith, again relying on the added play of a mystical tone. The wide smile that had loomed momentarily on mischievous lips ebbed as the shaman took in his unhappy surroundings. Propelled back to the very real, there was no longer a sense of play in his words as he began again, "I can see you are still curious. That is good; we can discuss it at length later, yet now is neither the time nor the place to discuss such things. Do you understand?"

"Yes, I guess so," muttered Vilmos. A chill traveled down his back again, mixed with confusion, for only a moment ago he had realized the two were playing with him.

Wandering the streets for a time and checking the wares at the different marketplaces occupied their time for a while until it seemed a sufficient time had transpired. Eventually the band came to stand before a large inn, one that looked very familiar to Vilmos, yet also unfamiliar; the dirtiness of the place disturbed him, but before he could object or comment, Xith paid the innkeeper. Wordlessly, they ascended the stairs to their rooms hoping to steal a few hours of much-needed sleep; exhaustion had finally eaten away the surge of energy that they had been feeling.

Considerably more sore the following morning or what he perceived as morning, his body aching everywhere, Vilmos stirred as his slumber was disturbed. Fortunately, however, he wasn't the only sluggish one, and the sun was high in the sky before they departed the inn. *High in the sky?*

Vilmos double-checked the sun's position again—low in the sky, he corrected himself; it was late afternoon, yet it never occurred to his weary mind that it was the same day. Quickly they sought out the garrison headquarters, which was located in the northern section of the city—a building that Vilmos immediately recognized. His heart thumped rapidly as they crossed a street, making for the unseen square that Vilmos knew was ahead.

Vilmos recalled the chance meeting with the remarkable bladesman oddly. The face he pictured as if he had seen it only yesterday, the tall form he had taken in that single panning glance, the sound of the gruff voice seemed a distant recollection, yet it was the voice that he recalled with the greatest fondness. He wondered if the competition were still underway; and in the excitement, his weariness ebbed and he asked a question that in retrospect he knew he shouldn't have. Xith's rebuttal, although brief, was particularly stinging; he was not to say another word until they were inside the garrison proper.

Noman slipped the sentry the customary bribe for admittance, which to his dismay was promptly refused. After that, it took both Xith and Noman nearly a full hour to convince the man that he should let them enter the outer keep and to send for the day captain. The man seemed particularly miffed at the attempted bribe, and it was only through persistent nagging that they were allowed entrance at all.

"Night cap'n's watch comin' on soon, ya' know," mumbled the squat man.

"Yo'all need to stay here," he added, disappearing into a hallway, an ironbound door clanging closed after him.

They had made it as far as the inner gatehouse and no farther. A portcullis lay between them and the outer keep and another to the rear insured that they were retained here until someone returned, which they hoped would be soon. Xith grew visibly angry as the day dwindled away and the captain hadn't come back. Even the steadfast Amir was getting edgy, his hand subconsciously fondling the hilt of his sword.

Vilmos was the only one who didn't mind waiting. He thought it was a good opportunity to talk with Noman; unfortunately Noman didn't think so. Noman was busy trying to confer with the guards, who suspiciously watched them. He repeated the same question concerning the day captain's whereabouts only to receive no response. The guards would only glare at him with disgust and contempt. He was tempted to use the guiles of the voice, but never quite did. The voice relied on a somewhat receptive audience and the guards neither paid attention to them nor cared if they were made to wait all day.

The captain finally arrived just after sunset.

"So, you're still here?" the captain said, acting surprised, "I do not have time to waste with the likes of you. I am off shift; you should consult the night captain if you still wish to speak with someone. Guards, dismiss them at once. Good Evening."

Noman put a quick end to diplomacy; his patience was at an end. "Good evening is all you are going to say after you have made us wait for the better part of the day?"

Better judgment prevailed and Noman withheld his anger. Time was running short; they should have been on their way already. "You are Captain Nijal, first son of Geoffrey. I would advise you to take me to see your father now or I'll have your head!"

The name brought instant remembrance to Vilmos and now he matched the broad shoulders hidden beneath padded armor with a distant visage he had briefly envied, the distant figure that had been one of the few in the respected group that had ascended from the field of combat to the lofty balcony to stand beside their lord. The words of the bladesman rang in his ears: "The test of steel lasted six days for that one." Vilmos waited to see how he would react to the challenge.

"You make demands here? I think not!" rebuked the captain.

Vilmos silently cheered, though not because the man was defying Noman, but because the words fit the image he held in his mind's eye.

"I think so," calmly stated Noman with a scowl. Noman made a reaching motion with his hands, twisting his fingers around an imagined globe and then clenching the fingers tight, destroying the globe. The captain fell to the ground, his face whitening with horror as he realized he was unable to move. "Have you looked to the heavens lately?"

Vilmos gulped, suddenly sorry for his wishes of defiance.

The sentries lunged forward and then stopped. Noman waved his hands again, a twinge of malice held in his upturned eyes, and the captain fell to his belly—the sentries made no further advances. To Nijal it seemed as if the earth had suddenly opened up to swallow him and he groveled insanely on the floor for a time before he looked upon the vision only he could see. Noman played with the man, seeming to enjoy the torment he caused. His companions saw nothing, yet they knew that somehow the diviner had caused the man to suffer.

"I am Noman, guardian of the lost children of the Father, Master of the City of the Sky. Light fire to your feet as you scamper back to your father with my message!"

To his utter surprise, the man held his ground, and then an odd thing happened. Though the terrified captain was unaware of it, a true smile lit the diviner's face, yet it was short-lived. "You have two choices, Nijal, son of Geoffrey." The words were spoken with a wintry tone as if each word cost the speaker pain and toil, "Draw the blade that you are so proud of, or do as I have instructed!"

Suddenly, as if he had just found that he had feet, the captain scrambled away, fleeing into the keep. He returned moments later with an older gentleman, nearly dragging the elder behind him. The old man's form spoke of one who had once been powerfully built but had softened with age. His voice was softened and gently aged.

"I am Geoffrey; please follow me," he stated, leading them away.

The words of the bladesman suddenly rang in his ears again. "He's been the best for a decade now, and the Father willing, I think he will make a comeback this year." Vilmos studied father and son, searching for the similarities between them, of which there were many, suddenly noting how young the other looked, and truly was, when compared to the older gentleman. Momentarily, he wondered if any man could match the powerful Amir in a test of steel; somehow, he didn't think so.

Two groups of escorts accompanied them on the brief walk through the keep. Captain Nijal directed wary glances solely at Noman, a worried expression forming on his face with each; it was clear that he was terrified of the mystic.

Vilmos glanced back at the small open yard with its covered overhangs and fountains as they passed into the inner keep. The rear guard lagged behind now as they paused to seal the doors and Vilmos paused likewise, turning to regard them. They were not outfitted like the outer sentries in padded leathers and helmet. They wore a shining chain, which was obviously lightly woven as they moved with ease, and an open-faced helmet with a long plume, a clump of black feathers, on its top. Their weapons were not pike and glaive, but full two-handed swords with fine hilts and ornate scabbards.

The brief walk ended when they entered what appeared to be a large audience chamber with a large, rectangular table with ten chairs on each long side and two chairs on the short sides filling most of it. Two of the sentries remained outdoors, but the other pair followed Geoffrey to the head of the table. They took up positions on either side of him.

Vilmos was curious now, for none of them had been searched for weapons. Was this because Noman played out an illusion before their eyes of a harmless band of peddlers, or was it because the lord knew without a doubt that no matter what occurred the two stalwart figures planted behind him would protect him regardless of the cost to themselves? He would have liked to believe the latter, for he took an odd liking to the young captain and his noble father.

Noman skipped any introductions and cut the conversation short by dropping an illusion, which he had obviously concocted and fine tuned during the short walk, into the center of the table they were now seated around. Little further explanation was necessary; Geoffrey fully understood the banners he saw raised.

Geoffrey and Nijal sat with eyes wide in disbelief at what they were witnessing. Yet true wonderment came when Geoffrey of Solntse recognized his own standard among the many raised on the illusionary field, for this small thing defined the intricacies in the precarious detail. Vilmos again noted that emotion did not stir the sentries' faces. They stared directly ahead without variance.

Noman did speak now, in kind, cognizant prose, emanating a feeling of peace and truthfulness, which overwhelmed even Vilmos. He continued to speak at length about things Vilmos had never heard him mention to anyone else, things that caused Vilmos to start and tremble. Words like war, death, famine, and suffering, that rang in his ears long after Noman finished.

Lord Geoffrey spoke for a time in a reasonable fashion that surprised some of the listeners. He seemed to have listened well, and it was clear that he intended to heed the warning. And then a strong silence permeated the room, lasting until the guardian cleared his throat and looked to Xith. The shaman smiled, looked to Geoffrey for a moment and then nodded his head; he was sufficiently satisfied with the other's intent to hold to his promise. Xith winked at the young captain as they broke from the table, causing the man to fidget.

They stopped at the open yard where Geoffrey offered them a place to stay for the night, which they declined, declaring that they must depart immediately. Nijal further offered them swift horses from the garrison's own stock, supplies for their journey, and his deepest apology, which Noman accepted.

As they reached the outer keep gate, the young captain made one final appeal to them to accept his father's and his own gracious invitation to stay the night. Guilt rode upon his shoulders for the way he had treated those that had been trying to help him; and this sat very uneasily with him, for he thought of himself as fair and not self-serving. "Is there any way we can further assist you?"

"No, we must be going. I am truly sorry," said Noman, patting the captain's shoulder.

Nijal looked to his father. He wanted to say something but couldn't. With Noman in their midst, the ruggedness of the newcomers was strangely appealing, yet he wondered why such a powerful man kept such poor company, or if perhaps there were more than was apparent. He watched the guardian as the outer portcullis was slowly raised and an unanticipated sadness came to him as he began to walk away.

Noman whispered to Nijal as they exited, "Things are not always as they seem, friend Nijal."

A small contingent of garrison soldiers waited with the fresh mounts. The group dismounted at their approach and it became quickly apparent to the onlookers that these where the soldiers' personal mounts. The animals were large, muscular, and obviously well groomed and maintained. Saddlebags were quickly brought out and distributed. And then since there was nothing more to say, Noman and the others quickly accepted the gift and departed. The two, father and son, watched the departure; again a curious sadness passed between them.

"Times are changing, my son," said Geoffrey.

"Yes, father, to think the guardian has left the fabled city."

"Life is breathed into the myth," added the lord.

"Indeed! Could you feel the power that emanated from him? He seemed larger than life itself. By my code, our code, one to be reckoned with."

"From the group, I would say," countered the lord.

"Father? May I—" began Nijal, adding remorsefully, "No, it is only a foolish notion."

"What is only a foolish notion?" inquired Geoffrey as he turned to face the young man.

The others were gone from sight now and the gate was grinding down with an unsettling whine. As the lord sauntered into the courtyard, his bodyguards followed and Nijal walked alongside him.

"I know they go to meet something important and all I can do is look around and see these dead, gray walls. I need purpose in my life, father. I need to find my freedom."

"Yes," said Geoffrey sighing. The final word had struck a chord and the words of the freeman's code flooded into his mind; it was all that he stood for, all that he wanted to maintain for his son. "Perhaps I have kept you here for too long. You were never one to stay in one place too long. Yet I thought I finally had satisfied you."

The lord sighed again and then continued, "You have a considerable position in the city, yet you are unhappy, you are not free. You are indeed my son."

Geoffrey's grim demeanor lessened.

"I am a free man."

"Yes, you are my son. Who would you have lead the garrison in your stead?"

"You know the one, Father. He is far better than I."

"You have trained him well. He will make a worthy captain."

"Shchander is a good man."

"Yes, he is."

"Then I have your permission?"

"Yes, go my son. Find what it is you seek so that someday you may return a settled man. May the Father watch over you!"

"And you as well, Father!"

Nijal rushed inside to gather a few of his scattered belongings; when he returned, his stallion was saddled and ready for him. The new captain stood next to Geoffrey and the three saluted each other in mutual respect as Nijal departed.

Hastily, he rode away, heading toward the eastern gates of the city. Still he could not believe his father had allowed him to leave. The life of a captain was definitely not for him. He needed excitement and change, which he hoped to find.

"What of the watch?" shouted Shchander, chasing after Nijal.

Nijal grinned and waved, saying nothing.

Soon the eastern gates lay behind him and the open plains of the border country stretched out before him. He wasn't sure to where he ran, only that the visitors had said they were headed eastward and so was he. He was a little disconcerted when he found no immediate sign of them or their passage, the dry earth showing no telltale dust plume of the retreating riders. He decided to ride east for a time.

He hoped his brash nature hadn't left him without a job for he could not return now, even if he wanted. He had already given his position as day captain of the city garrison away, or at least that was the thought that spurred him on. He cradled the stout leather whip in his hand and hastened his steed onward.

Dusk besieged the murky land and Nijal found himself squinting in the falling silvered light to find the thin trail that led to the east. Surrounded by a disturbing lull, mentally he keyed his senses, searching for the night sounds he knew should be there—the distant call of nocturnal hunters waking from a day's sleep, the scurrying of the border hare, a scrawny, thick-skinned rabbit that he found surprisingly tasty, or even the cry of the speckled black bird which abounded in the flat lands, a bird which the nomads called the gray raven.

Finding a few of those sounds in the distance after a time, Nijal no longer felt lost and alone, yet this was not why he persisted; it was as though an invisible hand were guiding him on, pulling him through the waning day and forcing him to ride on when otherwise he might have turned back.

He glared across the horizon, spotting the only things that marred the otherwise featureless land around him, small stands of stunted trees, trees that looked as if the sun never found them beneath the perpetual blanket of wind-blown debris tossed up from the rough lands by the coarse, damaging winds.

His pace slackened now, as he oddly lost the sense of urgency, yet the unseen hand still guided him on—he would never recall that he hadn't paused to look back at the grand city in the fading light. The night sounds served better than a pacifier in a child's mouth to soothe his agitated senses, and for a time he came to rely on them; that is, until they abruptly stopped. His first reaction was to rein in his mount, but then, feeling foolish, he urged the animal on.

Passing a small cluster of the sickly wood now, he stopped abruptly; once more, on the far side of the stand, mixing with the overshadowed land, silhouettes were outlined in the falling light as long mishappen shadows. His first thought was of bandits; they often waited in such places for unwary passersby.

Taking the reins in one hand, he groped for the pommel of his sword and eased it from its scabbard, yet as directly as he drew it, the fears dissolved. The guiding hand led him on, tugging him forward. Warily, he approached and when sufficiently close to make out faces within the gray, he stopped, ignoring the strong beckoning of the hand, lingering shortly, waiting purposefully.

"Welcome Nijal, first son of Geoffrey of Solntse," called out a strong voice.

Nijal recognized the voice as that of Noman, yet he didn't recognize the face.

"We have been waiting for you," commented the voice.

"How did you know I would come?" asked Nijal skeptically.

"You could not have done otherwise."

Noman introduced each of the group in turn; the titles of all save the young man, Vilmos, were quite impressive to behold, yet he did not mention the name of their most beautiful companion which left Nijal hanging as it became readily apparent that Noman was going to say no more.

"I would say it is a safe assumption that you know this country like the back of your hand. Is that not right, my young friend?"

Nijal gave a subdued nod of the head.

"We travel south my young friend, south toward the open country. Will you not lead the way?"

"But I thought you were headed east?"

"We have, perhaps, changed our minds," said Noman with a grin.

The group departed, turning a wide circle south and east, with a stunned young captain staring at the Gray Eagle Lord who had just launched effortlessly into the quickly darkening sky on powerful wings. Vilmos stole the opportunity to intercede on the other's behalf, saying, "Many strange things happen in this group, friend Nijal; in time it will all just seem natural, because to them, it is—"

"Quickly now!" hastened Noman, "We have one more to gather."

16

In the half-light of dawn, a long line of ships gathered. The serene sky returned to blue, the call of the gull filled the air, and moderate waves splashed against a rocky shore spraying a fine salty mist. Sailors, soldiers, free men, and mercenaries alike had begun their toil long before the dawn had come. There were two groups of vessels in the sea this day, the large three-masted sea vessels whose silhouettes hung long in the still shadowed day and a tiny fleet of longboats that forever shifted between ship and shore.

Seth looked on; it was a grand sight to him. It marked the return to his lands and his people and a chance for their survival. A temporary lull while the longboats returned once more to shore to ferry supplies allowed his mind to wander. Yet this didn't last long until he was interrupted by Cagan calling to him from the lower deck. The last of the stores were finally secured in the hold and it was time for those waiting to board. Lines formed and people filled the tiny boats to capacity the second they touched land. There was energy in the air, eagerness, a culmination, and an end to the waiting.

Satisfied with the proceedings, Cagan and Seth returned to shore, crossing the now barren fields on foot to the place where the last tent stood. Seth paused a moment in reflection. The field was strewn with debris and discarded goods. Although a few stragglers remained, Peddler Town was all but disbanded. Its dividing fence in shambles, the training field was also empty now.

The emptiness saddened Seth for a reason he couldn't understand. He didn't linger much longer; turning away, he flung the tent's door open and walked in. Chancellor Van'te, Keeper Martin, Father Jacob, the newly appointed captain, Evgej, and Prince Valam were already inside waiting.

The meeting was meant for the seven of them alone. They had decided previously that they would split up into two groups; the first would depart as soon as the meeting commenced and the second would follow at mid-day with the change of the tides. Father Jacob, Keeper Martin, and Captain Evgej would be on the lead ship of this second group, the others on the first lead ship.

The individual captains had already been given plans and contingencies in case any of the ships were separated. A primary point of arrival and a secondary point had also been designated on the maps they had distributed. This meeting was to firm up any loose ends they had previously overlooked and to set the plans into action.

Chancellor Van'te was to remain behind and wait for word from King Andrew. Finalizing the plans was a meticulous process accomplished only after long, exasperating minutes. A few minuscule items were found, nothing more. Next they discussed the chain of command from Valam down to the lowest of the ranking soldiers. They had no idea where the enemy would be, and this they discussed also. Goodbyes were said, and since there was nothing more to say, the companions parted ways. After the ship captains had been contacted and everything was in place, Captain Cagan hoisted the signal flag. His ship was the first to raise sail and embark. In pairs, the others followed in two drawn-out columns.

"A beautiful sight, I must say!" exclaimed Cagan, his love for the sea evident. The sight of ships on the horizon as far as he could see gave him a sense of elation.

"Yes, indeed!" answered Seth and Valam.

"I wonder how Evgej will fare with those two?" asked Seth.

"Keeper Martin will probably drive him mad by the time the journey is over, and Father Jacob will probably turn him into a convert. He'll be quoting whole sections from the Great Book," replied Valam with a jovial tone.

"Or bore him to death with their intellectual talks. I can see it now," joked Seth.

"Yes, that is probably what will happen. Poor fellow. I will miss him sorely."

"And I have lost my fencing partner," returned Seth.

"I don't think so," said a familiar voice from below.

"You are going to get us in real trouble," said Valam. "What will the men in the ranks think when they see you gone?"

The three turned and stared as Evgej climbed the ladder to the upper deck. Water dripped from his hair down his face and his tunic and leathers were clearly soaked.

"No trouble at all, I assure you. It was a simple solution really. You see—"

"You are all wet," said Seth as he looked at the water dripping from Evgej.

"A minor issue in truth."

"How did you manage to sneak away from them?"

"I didn't sneak. They both decided it would be best for me to accompany you. They said I could keep you three in line."

"Oh, really?" exclaimed Valam.

"Well, actually, it was because of—how did Father Jacob put it—oh, yes—I looked like a lost toddler when you departed. He said, 'If you are going to reach the ship before it departs you had better hurry.' I almost made it, too; however, I had to take a slight detour to get aboard. Lost my balance actually."

The four burst into raucous laughter.

"Come with me below; I'll get you some dry clothes," said Cagan.

With a final wave to the distant figure of Father Jacob, the two went below decks; Seth and Valam remained above. Valam had a broad smile on his lips; with the four of them together the journey would be anything but dull. Father Jacob watched the last of the first group depart, pairs of sails turning away, becoming smaller and smaller. He was rather eager to get underway, yet the changing of the tides was several hours away.

"Do you think it was a good idea to send Captain Evgej with those three?" asked Chancellor Van'te jokingly.

"I'm not so sure," answered Keeper Martin.

"All these men to fight away from their lands; most will never return. Is it all worth it?" asked Van'te. The question had been at the tip of his thoughts all day; he would not have asked it in the presence of the others. He knew Martin and Jacob would accept the question at face value and not dwell on it, so he had asked.

"If you had seen the images from Seth's home you would be convinced beyond any doubts. There will always be doubts in any endeavor, but in this the consequences far outweigh any doubts. I just wish we had heard from King Andrew beforehand, yet this was the date he himself set. I am anxious to know if the delegates have arrived from the Minor Kingdoms. Last night I sent a message to the council, but I am not sure if it was heard. My thoughts were in disarray with such a short time to prepare, and the distance is great. I may only hope."

"As do I. I have received no word from the priesthood. Still, I am confident we made the correct decision."

"Yes, Father Jacob, we were not given much choice in the matter. The situation has turned suddenly so serious. There is no doubt—we made the right choice."

They sat quietly contemplating their own thoughts; soon it was time to say their goodbyes also. They must depart now, for the tide had changed. The ships were fully boarded and now only one of the longboats remained. It waited at the shore, its four oarsmen weary from a day that had already been too long for them. Jacob didn't much care for ships or travel by sea and as he stepped into the small boat, he crossed himself and said a prayer to the benevolent Father to watch over him and keep him safe throughout the journey, which he hastily amended with a prayer for all who departed this day. His thoughts were especially with Prince Valam.

On Keeper Martin's command, the signal flag was hoisted. Their ship, the lead ship, was the first to raise its sails, tighten its lines, weigh anchor and make the long arcing turn for clear open waters. At mid-day the sea was broken only by a delicate ripple, but as the giant vessels began to glide through its dark waters it swelled and churned, as if offering a slight resistance. As the lead turned its sails fully westward, the others were making their exodus from the shore in a staggered array.

Chancellor Van'te watched the last pair grow to small specks on the horizon before he prepared to return home. The command tent was removed from the field, and now it was truly empty. Only one peddler stand remained.

The benevolent chancellor felt that he was indebted to the old man, though for what he did not know. He dismounted, a slow feat for the aged chancellor, and approached the small bit of canvas that served as a meager shelter from the rains and winds for the peddler and his wares.

"Good day to you, gent," said Van'te.

The peddler did not move. His head was slumped and his chin rested oddly on the top of his dirty coat. His hands were crossed, left over right and folded over his lap. Van'te noted the thick scent of mead from within the tent. At first, the chancellor thought the other was a drunkard, then he saw the many small oaken casks. His frown departed and the corners of his mouth lifted as he inhaled heavily of the sweet aroma.

"Good day to you, sir!" called out Van'te.

The peddler did not stir.

"Good day to you, sir!" he called out again.

The man was still as death, and for an instant, this notion crossed Van'te's mind. This idea that the man was indeed dead would seem an appropriate explanation for his lagging behind. Dying in a barren field was a bitter end. Van'te's sour countenance slowly crept back into place.

"How much for the lot?" The chancellor asked.

He lurched, expecting the old peddler to accept the offer eagerly. The chancellor signaled his attendant and turned back to his mount; gaining the saddle was as tedious a feat as departing it. He chased away offers of assistance; the day he could no longer take to saddle was the day he wished to pass like the old vendor, quietly and sadly where there would be no loved ones to see him go and feel the pain.

The small party headed by the chancellor began the solemn ride back to the city. The guardsmen seemed as touched by the incident as the chancellor had been. He flicked the reins, signaling his mount to go. He looked back, a long hard stare, as the animal beneath him raced forward. He was halfway to the city when his conscience forced him to turn around. He raced back to that empty field, just as his attendant and two others were preparing to lower the peddler's ragged tent.

"Leave it," he said, in a low voice.

"Leave it?" questioned the attendant.

"Leave it," the chancellor replied, "find his book of records, if he has one, and bring it to me."

"But—"

"That cache of mead smells of the finest sort in all the land and I would imagine that it is. What would you say would be the worth of such a treasure?"

"Nothing to a dead man."

"Return with a wagon, and bring me the record when you find it. Lay his bones to rest in this field only at peril of your own life."

The chancellor didn't know why he said this; but as he did, he whipped his reins and urged his steed to a full gallop. He rode back toward Quashan', uttering not a single word until he dispatched a messenger for the local keeper. Van'te had talked to him many times in the past few days; he grew to dislike the man more each time. Keeper Parren was a different man than Keeper Martin, extremely different. Still, he was the head keeper for their city, so he must be informed that the departure had taken place as set forth.

Keeper Parren awoke suddenly, snapped from his dream by an urgent-sounding summons at his chamber door. It took him quite a while to gather his thoughts. For a moment, he had thought he was back at home in Imtal. Slowly a picture began to form in his mind, the dream. The message was made faint and unclear by the sound of incessant thrashing at his door.

He was sure of one thing: something was very wrong in Imtal. He sat lost in a trance of remembrance, a trance that should have cleansed his mind and brought the message of the dream forth. The thoughts would not come, only a vague feeling that something was wrong, a picture of the palace at Imtal and a faint image of a man. He continued to follow his thoughts back through his sleep. The answer did not lie in his dreams.

He jumped from his trance as the pounding returned to the door.

"What is it?" he bellowed haughtily.

"A message, Keeper, from Chancellor Van'te," exclaimed the page, sounding urgent.

"For this you wake me as if the very earth were crumbling beneath my feet! For this you raise a heavy fist again and again to my door!"

The keeper didn't much care for the chancellor either, as was evident in his tone.

"Bring me the note, you oafish boy! Don't just stand there peering within! Boy, come here!"

The youngster inched forward warily.

"Don't just stand there; hand me the note, boy! The note—"

Keeper Parren read the message, muttering to himself about the summons. He chased the boy away with a violent hand gesture, quickly dipping his face in the basin beside his bed and then dressing in the appropriate robes of his office. He didn't race down the hall; instead, he walked at a moderate pace. Any other day he would have stopped off at the kitchens for a quick bite, but this day the strange dream gnawed at the corners of his thoughts.

He found Chancellor Van'te in the study, not in his office, oddly gazing out an open window. The keeper quietly approached, waiting until Van'te turned from the window before he said a word. The two spoke brokenly for a moment, the chancellor muttering something about sleeping past the midday and the keeper mumbling about dotards. Keeper Parren was quick to discuss the dream that pervaded even his waking mind. The two discussed this for a time and it puzzled them both. There must be a reason the message was sent, but they could not tell what it was.

"The man in the image—you couldn't see him?" snapped the chancellor.

"Just the outline of him superimposed over the castle. I assume it must be King Andrew."

"The king—that is odd," said Chancellor Van'te, his voice suddenly becoming mild as chagrin set in.

"I can think of only two reasons the Council of Keepers would send a message with such feelings: to have us stop the journey or to inform us of a happening of great import."

Keeper Parren decided to go into the dream-state again. Only this time, Chancellor Van'te would probe his thoughts as he recalled them with verbal cues—a trick he had learned from Martin and Jacob. He told Keeper Parren to delve back through his night's dream one step at a time, and slowly inch forward. The images rolled into Parren's mind at a rate that only his subconscious could perceive. Hours passed in minutes, or perhaps minutes passed in hours. Time held no bounds within his thoughts.

Van'te found a detail the keeper had overlooked. The image of the castle was hazy, but certain things could be noted. The gates of the castle were closed, and the kingdom flag was not flying. The chancellor broke the link immediately; now he understood. Keeper Parren continued the trance, slowly recovering from it until his mind was free.

Chancellor Van'te returned his stare to the open window and the small courtyard below it where the sun continued to shine and where it seemed that the entire world had been cleansed. Without a doubt, he understood the message, King Andrew was dead and the only heir to the throne of the Great Kingdom was gone.

17

Nijal and Vilmos had talked a lot since the former day captain of the Solntse City Garrison had joined their small band. The two found that they had a lot in common and shared a similar dream. They didn't strive to be wealthy or important; they just wanted to have purpose in their lives.

Vilmos explained much to Nijal, who always listened intently, about those of the mysterious company. The free man often felt he did not belong in such a group, a feeling that Vilmos shared with him since the departure of the wild magic, yet Vilmos assured him that if he did not belong he would not be here with them. And from those meager ties, their strange friendship grew.

Vilmos continued his tutelage under Xith's scrutinizing eye. Talk of the opposing forces had led to more in-depth discussions about the properties within those forces of positive and negative, sometimes viewed erroneously as good and evil—the four basic elements of fire, air, water, and earth. Since the boy had begun with fire, the simplest and the most powerful, and then gone on to air, a median power, Xith considered continuing on to the third element, water. However, he decided to hold off for a time and allow the young man more time for adjustment.

Air was a power that the young apprentice was already very familiar with, a power that he had often played with though he had not known it at the time, so this was where the shaman concentrated his efforts. He found that Vilmos easily understood the realm of air once he put it into a readily understandable context. Since levitation was a skill that relied on the realm of air and a skill that Vilmos had often tried though he had not known how to control it, Xith chose this skill to begin with.

As with the previous lessons, Xith only wished to impart to Vilmos one basic skill, a stepping-stone that would prove the basis for all other dealings with this property. Levitation was simply re-applying the powers he had touched on in the lesson with the rocks, a lesson that Vilmos uneasily recalled.

The journey to the city of Solntse had taken them days out of the way, but this was also a mixed blessing. Although the trek was lengthened by several days, they would not have to endure the tireless extremes of the high desert whose temperatures would roast them during the day and freeze them at night.

Amir rode beside his Little One; occasionally he attempted to carry on a conversation with her but mostly he seemed to be talking to himself.

He didn't mind, though. He could bathe in the beauty she radiated forever. He hoped eventually to find out her secrets and be able to alleviate some of her burden. Xith and Noman rode side by side though seldom a word passed between them. They were content to ride quietly, watch the countryside pass, and concentrate on the dangers that lay ahead.

Something troubled Noman deeply, yet each time he tried to grasp the thought it slipped from him. Xith and Ayrian had similar feelings, the sense that something was amiss; yet as surely as they tried to discern what it was, it slipped away from their thoughts.

This night they made camp a short distance from the main road. While they were well into the heart of the Great Kingdom there was little fear of incidents; nonetheless, they took precautions. They would each take turns at guard during the night. Vilmos was the unlucky one who was chosen to perform the first watch.

Vilmos didn't complain, though, because he knew they would each eventually get their turn. The long, dark night proved thankfully uneventful; Xith, who had taken the last watch, woke them just before dawn. A light breakfast was eaten and preparations to start on their way were made as the sun appeared on the horizon.

Nijal wiped his tired eyes and nudged Vilmos, who was slumped over seated upright.

"Wake up!" he implored.

Vilmos opened bleary eyes, astonished to find his hand half raised to mouth. He mumbled through a quick apology, cut short as a warning flashed out to all. Stand still, warned the voice in their minds. Noman hurriedly crafted an illusion to hide their presence from the unseen danger. No one dared to move, their eyes set on a place behind them on the trail. Shadows shifted across the land as partially seen clouds passed through the half-shrouded sky.

Under this canopy of darkness, an extremely large group of men clad in dark high-hooded cloaks approached on horseback, hoping to use even the last few moments of darkness to conceal their passage. Slowly, following Noman's signal, Xith and the others moved to their horses, moving away from the trail.

As they watched, the dark group stopped and made camp off the trail only a short distance away. The light of morning grew and the strangers seemed to disappear with its arrival, leaving no signs of themselves or their camp.

Noman signaled the party to move again; and they moved away from the mysterious group, pausing only to look back briefly, riding hard until the sun blazed fully overhead, only then stopping to discuss what they had seen. Nijal was more puzzled than worried and Vilmos' expression of confusion only added to the free man's befuddlement. He had seen groups of highwaymen before though never one so large.

"We must stay ahead of them. We have a long, hard journey to undertake. It lies ahead of us; there is nothing behind us now and there can be no turning back," spoke Noman, looking to their newest companion, "yet at least we now know who the enemy are."

"Enemy?" gasped Nijal and Vilmos in unison.

"Ayrian!" bellowed Xith.

"Yes, I'll go," replied Ayrian, dismounting. He tethered his mount to Xith's saddle horn in simple, quick fashion and departed with two long pumpings of his great wings.

Nijal stared in awe toward the departing Eagle Lord. Vilmos had explained the transformation to him, but it still captivated him. Ayrian became a symbol of power and beauty in the new form. And then, with a final look behind, they continued on their way, riding until they were sure they were far, far ahead of what lay behind them. No further discussion was made of the dark figures; and this night they would not camp in the open, for they no longer felt safe, and a guard was now a necessity.

Nightfall seemed to come too soon when compared to previous days; and before the travelers knew it, the sun was setting. Nijal drew first odds and his watch began as his companions drifted off to an uneasy sleep. No fire was made; as night fell, it was only the light of the heavens that allowed him sight, and every sound alarmed him. It wasn't that he was without experience in the woods or the open land that brought on his fright, but rather an unsettling chill that seemed to rest upon his own skin and the air he breathed.

Nijal had camped alone in the dangerous border country before and endured darker nights than this, yet this seemed somehow more frightening and more portentous. He made such a commotion pacing through the undergrowth that he awoke the shaman more than once. After the third time, tired of soothing Nijal's fears, the shaman took over the watch. Nijal felt so chagrined that he offered to take Xith's watch, which was to be the last one of the evening. Xith accepted.

When it came his turn to watch, Vilmos was also fairly agitated. The night sky had grown dark and unforgiving. Shadows moved in his thoughts, matching those of the land, causing him to draw his small blade and hold it at the ready. Two hours of darkness gave him plenty of time to think. His mind roved over many subjects, not really resting on anything in particular.

Vilmos was greatly relieved when his time was up and it was Amir's turn at watch. The warrior sat grimly and statue-like on an old stump for most of his two hours listening to the night sounds, passing off the watch to Nijal without question as he had been told, and only with the coming of dawn did the young captain's nerves settle. Early the next morning Ayrian found the camp, startling Nijal into a panic in the process.

"It is I," hissed Ayrian softly.

Nijal sheathed his sword.

"Sorry," he answered.

"For a moment I thought you were going to run me through," replied

Ayrian in jest.

The sound of voices awoke several others whose stirrings, in turn, woke all save Vilmos, whom Nijal took it upon himself to arouse. Ayrian began his report at first slowly and then hurriedly as he noted the diviner's anxious stares explaining lastly that the highwaymen had made camp about an hour's ride away.

"From the looks of them, they are very good. They leave no signs of their travel. They ride in total silence; even the hooves of their horses are padded. However, they are a small group; they could not hope to do much damage."

"Unless there are more groups, or some are already in waiting," said Noman. "I have received a vision in my dreams. It was a portent of things to come. I have seen the many paths we follow; soon they will merge, then only one path will remain. We must hurry. As I have said, there is one more we must find and only then will our circle be complete!"

"What do the highwaymen have to do with—" Nijal started to ask. He was silenced by a heavy grip on his shoulder.

"You will see, friend Nijal," said Noman, "for now it is best to say no more."

Another day passed and again night returned to the shadowed land. Ayrian did not return to their camp that night or the following morning. As they broke camp once more, the friends expected him to appear at any moment; when he didn't, the fears only compounded. Something must have happened to him—but what?

Vilmos and Nijal rode on either side of Xith, expecting him to have the answer; yet, lost in contemplation, the shaman said little the entire day except to tell the young apprentice to dwell on his lessons and not on things over which he had no control. He said nothing more until much later, words that caught Nijal oddly and by surprise and part of which still sang in his ears: "Even the greatest of Men can fall and often the lesser among you will prove tenfold your greater. Your place is here with us, Nijal of Solntse. You are part of us now. Cast your petty fears behind you."

"Vilmos," moaned Nijal, snapping out of his reverie as he lurched forward, "you're doing it again."

Vilmos looked to the former captain and his horse; the two were floating about a foot off the ground. The docile steed still unknowingly galloped ploddingly along.

"Sorry," said Vilmos, "it is just—well, I guess you could say, it's just nervous energy."

"I'd hate to see it when you were really agitated then!"

"Sometimes I forget. I didn't mean to," said Vilmos.

"That's okay. It is kind of interesting to ride a floating horse."

"*Really?*"

"Ah, Vilmos?" asked Nijal, looking imploringly to the other, "Could you put my horse back down, and—um—gently this time not like last time."

Vilmos gently brought the horse down. He tried to clear his mind, yet his thoughts returned continuously to the lessons he had learned from Xith: laying a spark of fire to the air, using the forces of the air to shield himself, turning those same forces into a tool with which he could lift himself or others off the ground to glide and float, the workings of the flow, and how to touch upon the most primitive of forces within nature.

Vilmos' life had completely turned around, turned upside down, and come back again. He had been propelled through the stages of boyhood into those approaching manhood by the strange powers of the forbidden magic. He didn't miss home or the past anymore; he lived for the future. He also wondered if Xith would ever teach him how to teleport; somehow he doubted the shaman ever would.

"Vilmos!" exclaimed Nijal louder than he expected. Now the entire party was looking at Vilmos. Xith's eyes opened wide as he looked at his pupil and a smile broadened across his lips. Vilmos had his hands extended, between the fingers of one hand a red ball of light blazed and in the other was a ball of blue-white energy.

Vilmos stared at his hands in surprise. He had been thinking about Xith's lesson on energy, positive and negative. His face turned red in embarrassment.

"I guess I was thinking out loud!" he exclaimed, "Sorry."

Vilmos rode glumly upon his horse the remainder of the afternoon, afraid to let his thoughts wander and Nijal could do nothing to change his demeanor. Eyes intermittently scoured the heavens, searching for signs of the Gray Eagle Lord. They rode for many exasperating hours after sunset this day, pressing the tired animals more than they should have.

There was a perceived sense of urgency now, for the dark travelers were surely on their way to the same destination that they themselves raced to. The mystic had followed this path to its end in his uneasy thoughts. They were being led now by forces stronger than those that had propelled them onward—the unseen hand of fate was leading them all and only it knew where at last it would leave them.

There were no sightings of the mysterious dark travelers during the night, which passed uneventfully, and the monotony of the previous days had at long last ended. High day found them in a small town, in which they unhappily obtained fresh mounts and food. Having to settle on nags, they would sorely miss the swift animals they were forced to leave behind. Several of the animals had thrown shoes and the village smithy had told them he had a backlog of several days. They took the nags without complaint and continued on. The city of Kauj lay just ahead and with the fresh steeds, they would reach it by nightfall. They were hopeful once more; finally, they would be able to stop at an inn and rest, a short reprieve long overdue.

Vilmos and Nijal conversed on and off throughout the day. They had come to an area of hills sparsely populated with small stands of trees, remnants of the immense forests that had once stretched coast to coast and now only ranged sparingly throughout the Great Kingdom. The Belyj Forest, many leagues to the south, was the largest stand that remained of the great forests in the civilized realms—a forest as old as the land itself. In other sections of the land, far to the east and south, forests still dominated the land, populated by growths that were thousands of years old. It was odd yet somehow suiting, reflected Nijal, who was an infant in the eyes of the great oaks he now passed.

Noman eyed the young man with a knowing grin upon his face and then turned to the giant beside him. Amir was clearly agitated. He stretched and flexed his muscles ceaselessly, often uncoupling his great blade from his pack and casting it about the air. Time passed and Noman turned back to Nijal who was also restless.

Noman saw something in the young man's eyes that told him he would be ready when the test came. He wondered if the former day captain had any idea what sort of a quest he had agreed to with that simple desire to find purpose in life—so much lay ahead, and so very little lay behind. The journey to the path's end could take him through his lifetime, maybe even beyond. One never knew for sure. The diviner retreated from such thoughts, reflecting upon the converging paths for a time, finding irony that their meeting seemed so near.

"This is a city?" said Nijal questioningly as they approached the outskirts of the tiny city of Kauj, which in his eyes was little different from the village they had left behind the previous day.

"Yes, it is; I like small cities," said Vilmos. The shaman grinned.

The six companions approached the narrow row of structures that lined the main thoroughfare at a slackened pace an hour past dusk just as the last of twilight faded from the unseen horizon. It was beneath this canopy of darkness that the six passed along the shadowed streets of Kauj.

Lamplight cast its burnt-orange hues into the darkened streets here and there, and along the innermost throughways the odor of the burning oil wafted to their nostrils. The city was mostly quiet, and it almost seemed as if the entire population of Kauj was fast asleep. Yet there were shadows in the doorways every now and again, and sometimes whispers passed out into the street, carrying to their ears even above the soft plodding of the horses' hooves.

The group soon found the inn the shaman had sought out. It was true that it was not the large, well-lit establishment they had passed on the outskirts of the city along the main street; but cast in the orange of the lamplight, its sight seemed somehow reassuring and pleasant enough. They took the last two rooms the tiny inn had to offer—Xith, Vilmos and Nijal in one, and Noman, Amir and the Little One in the other.

The rooms were surprisingly spacious, so three occupants did not overcrowd them. The inn even had a bathing room, which the group immediately put to use. And it seemed for a short time that all was well.

Vilmos had almost faded off to sleep when Nijal plopped down on top of him. The youth instantly reacted and sent the free man flying to the ceiling, letting him cling to it for a time, playing with him.

"Come on, let me down. I was only kidding," pleaded Nijal.

"Not just yet," said Vilmos through a yawn, again playing with the other, "I think I'll leave you hanging up there while I go back to sleep, so I can listen to you drop onto the floor sometime in the night when I forget you are up there and my subconscious wanders."

"You wouldn't? You couldn't?" tested the former captain.

"I might," said Vilmos feigning another yawn, "just to see if I can do it."

"I'm sorry, okay, I'm sorry."

"For what?" chuckled Vilmos.

After a few more minutes, he finally decided to let Nijal down and was slowly lowering him to the floor when Xith entered the chamber. Xith's presence caused Vilmos to lose his concentration and Nijal fell to the floor with a thud. The two tried to look innocent, but Xith knew better.

"Great," he said, "since you have so much energy, then I take it you are ready to practice."

"Practice?" muttered Vilmos, expressing his displeasure with a sour grimace. "Why must I practice things that my other self already knows?"

Nijal looked sympathetically toward Vilmos; instead of a much-needed rest, Vilmos would practice. He shrugged his shoulders and then ambled over to his bed, looking sympathetically to his comrade just before he plopped onto the soft, quilted covers.

১৩৫ In the Service of Dragons ১৩৫

Vilmos didn't mind the practice; rather, he looked forward to it, and at first Nijal tried to stay awake to watch and listen. But despite his fascination, he slowly fell asleep. Teacher and apprentice settled in for a long conversation, both knowing neither would get much sleep this night. There were things the shaman needed to impart to the youngster before it was too late, lessons that needed to be learned and practiced, and lots more.

✻ ✻ ✻

Noman had left to take a bath, leaving Amir and the other alone. She looked so incredibly beautiful as she lay on the bed staring wide-eyed at the ceiling, hair brushed back and draped, still damp, over the fluffed pillow beneath her head. Amir could only watch her, wanting to say something to her, yet the words would not come out.

Amir's attentions were not lost on the Little One, and after a time she turned and stared at him. She wondered why he cared so much for her. She had done nothing but avoid him. Despite herself, a smile touched her lips, which Amir mistook as a sign. He went to her and knelt on the floor beside her bed, reaching out and taking her tiny hands into his.

"Amir, no!" she cried out, tears flowing down her cheeks.

She turned and faced the opposite direction. "Leave me alone!"

Amir walked over to his bed, slumped onto it and soon fell asleep.

The Little One eventually turned over and found herself staring back at the grim-faced warrior. "Why do you think you love me?" she whispered into the empty air, wanting to understand the strange infatuation.

Noman had returned from his bath and was standing in the doorway when her whisper broke the empty air. Instead of entering, he continued past the door, entering the next room along the short hall. Xith and Vilmos were still avidly discussing magic, and so he joined in.

"Noman," said Xith looking up, "good. I was just about to discuss your art with Vilmos. Now I have an expert to do that for me."

"I was more interested in hearing you teach Vilmos magic, but I will if you are interested."

"Yes!" exclaimed Vilmos.

"The art of creating illusions is a shading of the arcane arts. Once there were many principal forms of the mystic arts, so many wonderful shadings." There was a genuine affection held in the spoken words that brought a smile to both listeners' lips as the emotion touched off fond remembrances. "Times are changing and most have been lost. Of the multitude that once existed, only three forms remain.

"Will and Magic are the two basic forms from which all the others stem. Will uses the mind as your center to channel the natural energies of the world, the power of the trees, the strength of the wind, the rain, the flow of a river, the call of the land, of all nature. In this form, you focus these energies through yourself.

"As with all things, the amount of energy you may focus at any one time is dependent on the strength of your individual will power." Noman said this as a sort of note.

Neither listener minded; both had come to understand through their many talks together that the diviner sometimes tended to ramble and follow tangents. Yet they weren't prepared for the ominous ring of the words that would come next.

"Magic is quite different. Magic uses the energies of creation. Wild energies once proliferated. The Northern Range once held volcanoes that spewed new life continually, wild and fierce, and utterly devastating. The northern mountains now lie dormant, awaiting a return to the beginning. The energies of creation spring from the heavens, the stars, and the nether realm. The user of such powers is a thief."

Xith couldn't resist the temptation to interject, "Thief is such a strong word."

Noman glared and then smiled, continuing on as if the shaman had never said a word, "Stealing, devouring the energies of creation, robbing the future of new life, forever tied to the wild energies of creation and destruction, positive and negative you could say—of fire and earth, and of water and air. It is true that these forces seem similar to those that a user of will shapes; but, you see, the user of will shapes these forces as with a tool that is his center, bending them and molding them only temporarily. Yet the user of magic taps the destructive powers, the wild energies. These energies, once used, are spent.

"Yet the amount of energy you may use is also dependent upon your center. Only few are able to tap into this. You are one and the watcher is another.

"Illusion is similar to both magic and will. A person who creates illusions also has limited use of both will and magic. They combine these two skills, yet they cannot use external energies, only that which is within them, that which is at their center. An illusion is solely in the mind of its creator and by projecting these thoughts into others' minds they become seemingly real."

"Ouch!" exclaimed Vilmos.

"See, you felt the heat image I sent you. The visage of fire!"

"Yes, that is interesting," said Vilmos rubbing his hand.

"So all three are dependent upon your center?" asked Nijal.

The three looked to Nijal with evident surprise to find him awake.

"I thought you were asleep or I would have explained in more detail," said Noman.

"That is fine. Vilmos had already explained magic to me once. What do priests and priestesses use then? Is that magic?"

"No, that is a gift."

Nijal didn't quite understand. "Huh?"

"They are linked to the Father and the Mother. They get their powers in a totally different way, unrelated to the powers of any magic."

"These powers do not frighten you?" inquired Noman of Nijal, interested in the response.

Nijal mulled over the question for a while before responding.

"I would be a liar if I told you they didn't, yet while most of my brethren live in fear of things we do not understand, my father taught me to look for understanding first before passing judgment. So I would tell you that I am still passing judgment, and that I have not yet decided."

"Your father is a wise man," said Noman.

The four sat up talking for a short while more, each in turn retiring when sleep entered their eyes. They would need to get an early start in the morning, and it was getting late. Xith did, however, get in his objection one last time; and having the final say, he seemed pleased enough to be willing to go to sleep. Nijal was the last to fall asleep. He wondered if he would ever be able to do something special like the others; and he couldn't help but think about the words that Xith had spoken to him: "Even the greatest of Men can fall and often the lesser among you will prove tenfold your greater. Your place is here with us, Nijal of Solntse. You are part of us now; cast your petty fears behind you."

✳ ✳ ✳

Startled, Vilmos awoke, a scream sought to issue from his lips, but a man dressed terrifyingly in all black had a hand tightly clasped over his mouth. He strained to break free, yet could not; the man was too powerful and held him pinned in place. His eyes widened and he rapidly scanned the room for signs of the others. He was alone and one of the highwaymen had found him. His first notion was of defense. *Could he break free? Could he organize his scattered thoughts? Could he find the magic in time?*

"Calm yourself," whispered his assailant. "Here, put these on."

Momentarily, the voice didn't register with Vilmos; he struggled regardless.

"Calm yourself," the man repeated. "Put this on."

Vilmos sighed and shook his head to ward off the sleep-induced stupor, relieved that he recognized the voice.

"It is only an illusion; look again," hastened the voice.

Vilmos started to say something, but the hand remained over his mouth. He peered around the room again, this time less frantically. He saw Nijal across the room hurriedly getting dressed and did likewise. He quickly joined the others in the hall, noticing everyone was dressed in macabre hues. Noman restored the illusion then; Vilmos only knew this because he noted a subtle thought entering his mind—the watchword of an illusion's enactment.

As before, though, he saw no change in the appearance of the others—Noman had explained that this was because he knew the truth of what they really were, and illusions held no bounds over such truths. In hushed tones, Noman explained that Ayrian had finally returned with distressing news and they must leave immediately and secretly.

Flight from the inn was made with haste; the final race had begun.

Outfitted in dreary garb, it seemed they chased the dark wind, which howled unsettlingly. A chill came over Vilmos as they exited the city, the surrounding countryside hung with so many shadows that the land itself seemed utterly dreary and grim. And only then did the desperate flight and the desperate race seem real.

"One more to gather before we are through and then we have only begun," were the ominous last word's that Noman whispered into the wind— words that Vilmos dwelled on even though he had heard a similar utterance before because again they only sounded real just then.

End Of Book One

The Story continues with:

In the Service of Dragons II

Even now the dark forces gather.

Map of The Reaches

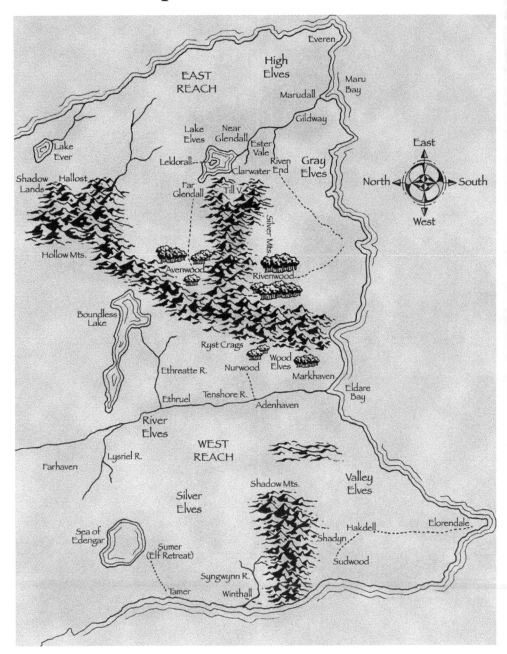

Everen

High
Elves

EAST
REACH

Maru
Bay

Marudall

Gildway

Lake
Elves

Near
Glendall

Ester
Vale

East

Leklorall

Riven
End

Gray
Elves

North ◄ ►► South

Lake
Ever

Clarwater End

West

Shadow
Lands

Hallost

Far
Glendall

Till V.

Silver Mts.

Hollow Mts.

Avenwood

Rivenwood

Boundless
Lake

Ryst Crags

Ethreatte R.

Nurwood

Wood
Elves

Markhaven

Eldare
Bay

Ethruel

Tenshore R.

Adenhaven

River
Elves

WEST
REACH

Lysriel R.

Farhaven

Valley
Elves

Shadow Mts.

Silver
Elves

Hakdell

Elorendale

Sea of
Edengar

Shadyn

Sumer
(Elf Retreat)

Sudwood

Syngwynn R.

Tamer

Winthall

Map of The Kingdoms

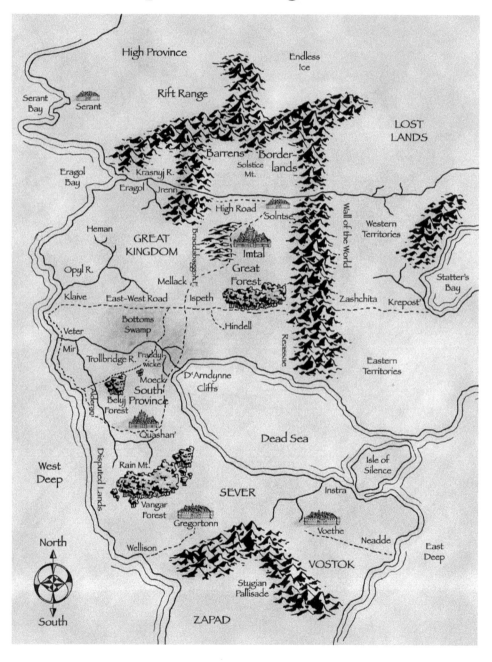

Meet the Characters

Adrina Alder
Princess Adrina. Third and youngest daughter of King Andrew.

Amir
Son of Ky'el, King of the Titans.

Andrew Alder
King Andrew. Ruler of Great Kingdom, first of that name to
reign.

Ansh Brodst
Captain Brodst. King's Knight Captain.

Calyin Alder
Princess Calyin. Eldest daughter of King Andrew.

Delinna Alder
Known as Sister Midori after joining the priestesses.

Jacob Froen d'Ga
Father Jacob. First minister to the king. Head of the priesthood
in Imtal.

Jarom Tyr'anth
King Jarom, ruler of Vostok, East Warden of the Word.

Mark
King Mark. The Elven King of West Reach.

Martin Braddabaggon
Keeper Martin. A lore keeper and head of the Council of Keepers.

Noman
Keeper of the City of the Sky.

Sathar
The dark lord.

Seth
Elf, first of the Red, protector of Queen Mother.

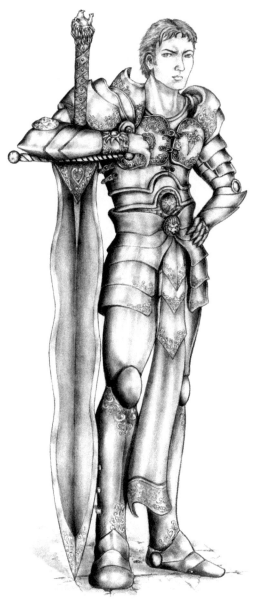

Valam Alder
Prince Valam, only son of King Andrew.

Vilmos Tabborrath
An apprentice of the forbidden arcane arts.

Xith
Last of Watchers.

Yi Duardin
Chancellor Yi . First adviser to King Andrew.

People, Places & Things in Ruin Mist

2 (2ⁿᵈ Alliance – 2ⁿᵈ Siege)

2ⁿᵈ Alliance   Alliance negotiated by Imsa Braddabaggon. Under the treaty Hindell, Ispeth, Mir, Veter and Solntse are protectorates of Great Kingdom but outside Great Kingdom's rule. The alliance was originally negotiated to stop the infighting between rival factions in these free city states and end bandit raids that were used to finance the fighting. The alliance includes trade and defense agreements.

2ⁿᵈ Siege   The 1,000-year siege of Fraddylwicke by Dnyarr the Greye. "Dnyarr the Greye, the last great Elven King, laid siege to Fraddylwicke Castle two times during the Race Wars in his attempt to gain the southlands. The first siege lasted over one hundred years, which wasn't enough time for young elves to grow to maturity but was generations to the men who defended the fields with their blood and their lives. Yet if such a thing was unimaginably horrible to endure for those who served, could one possibly imagine a thousand years of such as was the case of the last great siege?" – From the *History Of Fraddylwicke & D'Ardynne*.

A (Abrikos – Azz)

Abrikos   A walled city of Shost. Noble families: Ckrij, Triaren.

Adrina Alder   Princess Adrina. Third and youngest daughter of King Andrew. Her black hair and high cheekbones are from her mother as are the warm, inviting eyes. (See illustration)

Adrynne	A swamp in the southwestern part of Greye. In ancient Greye, Adrynne was a lady of high standing and was also the traitor of Shost.
Adylton, Captain	See Imson Adylton.
Aelondor	Father of Galan, of the Lake Elves of Near Glendall.
Alder	The Royal House of Great Kingdom. A reference to the Alder or the Alder King usually points to Antwar Alder, first king of Great Kingdom.
Alexandria Alder	Queen Alexandria. Former Queen of Great Kingdom; Adrina's mother, now deceased.
Alexas Mytun	King Alexas, ruler of Yug, South Warden of the Word.
Alexia D'ardynne	Champion of the Old World. Kingdom lore says that she was a human slave who seduced the most powerful elf king of all time, Dnyarr the Greye, and later gave birth to bastard twins, Aven and Riven. See Aven & Riven.
Amir	One of the lost. Child of the Race Wars. Son of Ky'el, King of the Titans.
Andrew Alder	King Andrew. Ruler of Great Kingdom, first of that name to reign.
Ansh Brodst	Captain Brodst. Former captain of the guard, palace at Imtal. King's Knight Captain.
Antare	A place of legend.
Anth S'tryil	Bladesman S'tryil is a ridesman by trade but a bladesman of necessity. He is heir to the Great House of S'tryil.
Antwar Alder	King Antwar. The Alder King. First to rule Great Kingdom.
Armon	Said to have been the greatest shipwright that ever lived. His designs for merchant galleys and war galleons are the most duplicated in the kingdoms. He is credited with the discovery of the Mouth of the World during the maiden voyage of Midnight Star, a war galleon constructed for the Alder's fleet. In truth, a misunderstanding between Armon and the ship's captain is more likely responsible for the discovery. During an argument between the shipwright and the

captain, the galleon crashed into the Jrenn Cliffs. The ship was supposed to have been dry docked at Jrenn, transported over the ground to the other side of the cliffs, and put back into the river so as to complete the voyage. The crash, however, broke through the rocks of the cliffs and into an enormous river cave. Being pigheaded, Armon insisted that they go out the other side of the cave the same way they had gone in. Crashing into the rocks a second time crushed the galleon's hull but the ship didn't sink until several hours later—enough time for Armon to claim the discovery.

Armore	Lands to the north of Greye.
Ashwar Tae	The 12th son of Oshowyn.
Aurentid	Ancient stronghold of old.
Aven & Riven	Twin sons of Alexia D'ardynne who rebelled against the tyranny of their father Dnyarr the Greye and helped liberate the kingdoms. Aven and Riven were denied their birthright as one of the Greye, and took no last name that is known. Aven became the great intellectual of his time but as he kept mostly to the affairs of elves, little is known of him. Riven, on the other hand, renounced the throne of Sever though King Etry Riven I, a descendent of his line would later claim the throne.
Ayrian	Eagle Lord of the Gray Clan.
Azz	Village under protection of Daren.

B (Bandit Kings - Br'yan)

Bandit Kings	Rulers of the 12 clans of Oshowyn. Their people inhabit the Barrens, Borderlands and the mountains of the Rift Range. Their lands once extended to Ispeth and the Great Forest before they were driven north by the Alder King.
Barrens	Lands of desolation; desert near the western sea. "Beyond High Road is a vast desert called Barrens, a no man's land. Beyond the Barrens is the untiring Rift Range—ice-capped mountains of jagged black rock that climb perilously into the heavens."
Beast	Dark Lord, enemy of Amir.

Belyj Forest	Vast woodlands to the north of Quashan'. Named after Enry Belyj, the White Knight.
Berre, Captain	See Garette Berre.
Between	A dark, cold place through which realm travelers must go. "That place between worlds where the souls of the dead lingered before they passed beyond this life. That place without dimension that a mage can use to transition between realms."
Beyet	A walled city of Daren. Noble families: Shryth, Styven. War Lords: Lionne, Yras.
B'Him	Village under protection of Daren.
Bloodlord	A Ruler of Right and Knight of the Blood; one of the Nine Sons of the Blood.
Bloodrule	Commander of the blood soldiers, often called Father of the Blood. Less commonly called Tenth Son of the Blood.
Blood Soldiers	King Jarom's elite soldiers, born of the Blood Wars. "Too brutal and uncivilized for the civilized world that emerged after the Great Wars and too many to exterminate, they are all but forgotten about by both the kingdom that gave them birth and the kingdom that conquered them." (See illustration)
Blood Wars	Sometimes referred to as the last great war. It is the war during which Man drove the brother races out of the Kingdoms.
Borderlands	Lands situated between the Great Kingdom and the Northern Reaches. A wild, free country.
Bottoms	Swamplands in northernmost part of South Province. "There's things in there without names, but they'll try to take you just the same. They don't call it the bottom of the world for nothing. Fog rolls in so thick by mid-afternoon that you can't see your hand in front of your face."—Emel Brodstson.

Proper name is Fraddylwicke Swamp. See also Fraddylwicke.

Braddabaggon Hill country around Imtal. Imsa Braddabaggon as Head of Lore Keepers helped negotiate the 2nd Alliance.

Brodst, Captain   See Ansh Brodst.

Br'yan, Brother   Elf of the Red order. Proper Elvish spelling is Br'-än.

C (Cagan – Ckrij)

Cagan   Sailmaster Cagan. Elven ship captain of the Queen's schooner. Proper Elvish spelling is Ka'gan. (See illustration)

Calyin   Alder Princess Calyin. Eldest daughter of King Andrew.

Catrin Mitr   Sister Catrin. Priestess of Mother-Earth.

Charles Riven   King Charles, former ruler of Sever, North Warden of the Word.

Ckrij   A valley in the Samguinne Mountains; the founder of the city of Qerek and the first to discover the mystic minerals.

D (Dalphan – Dtanet)

Dalphan   The Wanderer; one of Great Father's first sons; he that created true death.

Damen   First kingdom of Greye; the ruling power of Greye.

Danyel' Revitt   Sergeant Danyel'. Former Sergeant Quashan' garrison.

Danyel' Tae	Son of Ashwar.
D'Ardynne	Cliffs formed where the Fraddylwicke Swamp and the Trollbridge River edge toward the Dead Sea. Although there is a Kingdom Road along the cliffs, the path is treacherous due to frequent rock slides and wet earth.
	Alexia D'Ardynne, a human slave for whom the cliffs are named, is a Kingdom heroine. Kingdom Lore says that Alexia seduced Dnyarr the Greye and gave birth to bastard twins, Aven and Riven half-elven, who would later help liberate the kingdoms. Sadly, it is also said that Alexia met her end on the very cliffs for which she is named.
Daren	Second kingdom of Greye.
Dark Priests	Also known as Priests of Dark Flame. A sect of priests, officially unsanctioned by the Priests of the Father and the Priestess' of the Mother, that work to expunge magic from the world. They were formed by universal decree after the Blood Wars by the then rulers of the Kingdoms and are not subject to the laws of the land or the rule of Kings. Their decrees are irrefutable laws. According to their law, magic use is a crime punishable by death and all magic creatures are to be exterminated. "Vilmos shuddered at the mention of the dark priests. Their task was to purge the land of magic, a task they had carried out across the centuries."
Davin Ghenson	Captain Ghenson. Imtal garrison captain.
Dead Sea	Lifeless sea to the east of South Province wherein lies the Isle of Silence.
Delinna Alder	See Midori.
Der, Captain	See Olev Der.
De Vit, Chancellor	See Edwar De Vit.
Dnyarr	Father of Daren, Damen, and Shost. The last great Elf King of Greye, creator of the four orbs.
Dream Message	One of the artifacts discovered by the keepers revealed to them the secret of sending messages across great distances (and it is rumored time). The keepers have used this knowledge as a way for the council and keepers spread

throughout the lands to communicate efficiently. In most cases, dream messages are received when a keeper is sleeping and can contain images as well as spoken words. Sending words requires great strength and close proximity. "To begin you must clear all thoughts from your mind and reach into the center of your being. A spark of power lies there that is your soul. You reach out with that power until you touch the consciousness of the one you wish to communicate with. You speak through images and feelings that you create in your consciousness." "It takes an extremely powerful center to create a vision in the form of thoughts that enter another's awareness as audible words. The simpler form is to use images and feelings."

Dtanet	A walled city of Shost.

E (East Deep - Evgej)

East Deep	The great eastern sea.
Eastern Reaches	East Reach. The realm of Queen Mother.
Ebony Lightning	Champion stallion, given to Emel Brodstson by King Andrew Alder for his service to the crown.
Edwar De Vit	Chancellor De Vit. King Jarom's primary aid and chancellor.
Edward Tallyback	A troant (half troll, half giant) and friend of Xith's. Edward would be the first to tell you that he is only distantly related to the hideous wood trolls and that he is a direct descendant of swamp trolls.
Edwar Serant	Lord Serant. Husband to Princess Calyin. Governor of High Province, also called Governor of the North Watch.
Efrusse, Efritte	Rivers; the two sisters. Efritte was in love with a nobleman from Beyet, but her sister, who disliked the nobleman, refused to let her sister wed him. So now as the river Efritte flows sadly down from the mountains, gradually gaining strength, momentum and hope, Efrusse jumps into the river and stops her, and is herself carried away by the river.

Efryadde The last Human Magus. Efryadde perished in the Blood Wars.

Elthia Rowen Queen Elthia. Former queen of Vostok, now deceased.

Eldrick A tree spirit of old.

Emel Brodstson Emel. Former guardsman palace at Imtal; Son of Ansh Brodst. (See illustration)

Endless Ice Uncharted lands north and east of High Province.

Enry Stytt Sergeant Stytt. A sergeant of the Imtal garrison guard.

Entreatte Former Capital of Greye, a city of Shost. Noble families: Jeshowyn, Khrafil.

Eragol Kingdom port town located where Krasnyj River meets the West Deep. Eragol is one of the Great Houses. Family Eragol is headed by Peter Eragol, Baron of Eragol.

Eran, Lieutenant See Tyr Eran.

Erravane Queen of the Wolmerrelle.

Etri Hindell Fourth son of Lord Martin Hindell. Family Hindell has wealth but little power in the kingdoms.

Etry Klaive Knight, husband to Ontyv and father of Etry II.

Etry Riven I Legendary King of Sever. He led an army of peasants and sword sworns to victory against Elven marauders.

Etry Solntse First Lord of the Free City of Solntse.

Everelle, Brother Elf of the Red order.

Ever Tree The oldest living thing in all the realms. It is the tree that helps Vilmos and guides him from Rill Akh Arr. "It was an odd-looking tree perched atop a rocky crag. The roots, stretching over rocks and gravel to the rich black earth a hundred yards away, seemed to have a stranglehold over the land and the trunk, all twisted and gnarled, spoke of the silent battle the tree was winning. Thick boughs stuck out from the trunk and stretched at odd angles to the heavens, almost seeming to taunt those that traveled below as their shadows lengthened with the waning of the day."

Evgej, Captain   See Vadan Evgej.

F (Faryn Trendmore – Francis Epart)

Faryn Trendmore   Captain Trendmore. Imtal garrison captain.

Faylin Gerowin   Huntsman Gerowin, a journeyman class hunter who is perhaps more than he seems.

First Brothers   Council made up of the presiding members of each order of the Elven Brotherhood.

Fraddylwicke   Barony also known as the Bottoms, formerly the gateway to South and home of Blood Soldiers. Fraddylwicke's inhabitants are the ancestors of King Jarom's Blood Soldiers.

Fraddylwicke, Baron   See Riald Fraddylwicke.

Fraddylwicke, Baroness   See Yvonne Fraddylwicke.

Fraddylwicke, Castle   During the Great Wars the castle was a major strategic point for King Jarom the First.

Francis Epart   Father Francis. Member of the priesthood of Great Father.

G (Gabrylle – Greye)

Gabrylle   A training master in Imtal.

Galan, Brother Elf of the Red order, second only to Seth. (See illustration)

Galia Tyr'anth Direct descendent of Gregor Tyr'anth. She is a king cat rider, bonded to Razor since the age of 12.

Gandrius & Gnoble Tallest mountains in the Samguinne. Gandrius and Gnoble were the ancient defenders of Qerek. Legend says that in the end, only the two held the Ckrij Valley from the Rhylle hordes. They are never tiring.

Garette Berre Captain Berre. A garrison captain in Quashan'.

Garrette Timmer Young guardsman, Imtal Palace. Son of Swordmaster Timmer.

Gates of Uver These mystical gates were once used to travel between the realms. In all, there are believed to be 7 gates fashioned by the Uver from a magic substance once mined from the deepest, darkest reaches of the Samguinne. Each gate is fashioned for a different purpose and a different kind of traveler. Two gates are recorded in the histories of Man. The gate in the Borderlands, fashioned for Man, is opened with the following words of power: *"Eh tera mir dolzh formus tan!"* The only other known gate is located in the Twin Sonnets. Both gates are masked from the world by a veil of illusion.

Geoffrey Solntse Lord Geoffrey. Lord of the Free City of Solntse. Descendant of Etyr Solntse, first Lord of Solntse.

Geref, Brother Elf of the Red order.

Ghenson, Captain	See Davin Ghenson.
Gildway	Ancient waterway in East Reach, flows from mouth of Maru Bay to Clarwater Lake.
Great Book	Book of Knowledge, used by Councilors of Sever and other southern kingdoms to relate the lore and the legends of old. The councilors and their families are some of the few commoners who can read and write. "Listening is the councilor's greatest skill. Each tale, each bit of lore, tells a lesson. Relate the lesson through the lore; it is the way of the councilor. Choose the wrong tale, give the wrong advice." "Books are a rare, rare thing in the land. It takes years, lifetimes, to pen a single tome. And only a true book smith can press scrolls into such a leather binding as befits the Great Book."
Great Father	Father of all. He whom we visit at the last.
Great Forest	Extensive span of forest south of Solntse.
Great Kingdom	Largest of the kingdoms, formed after the Race Wars. Referred to as *the Kingdom*.
Great Western Plains	Boundary between East and West Reach.
Greer	Alias for Anth S'tryil.
Gregor Tyr'anth	One of the greatest heroes of Sever and a martyr. Brother of King Etry Riven II.
Gregortonn	Capital of the Kingdom of Sever. Gregor Tyr'anth, for whom the city is named, was the brother of King Etry Riven II.
Greye	Land in Under-Earth where the three kingdoms were formed.

H (Heman – Human Magus)

Heman	Kingdom village; one of the oldest Great Families. The family matriarch is Odwynne Heman.
	Although no longer one of the Great Houses, Odwynne Heman does have a sponsor in High Council and does contest the revocation of title at every opportunity.

High Council, East Reach	Represents the elves of East Reach. Its members are the elves of noble families, which include those that are members of the Elven Brotherhood.
High Council of Keepers	12-member council of scholars that track the lore of the lands and are responsible for caring for the ancient artifacts. The council is headed by Martin Braddabaggon, also known as Keeper Martin. Keeper Martin has an arcane staff that allows him to teleport from Imtal to the High Council of Keepers, which is hidden in a secret location. Although the council is itself neutral, the council has aligned itself with Great Kingdom since the time of the Blood Wars.
High Hall	Meeting chamber in the Sanctuary of the Mother, East Reach.
High King's Square	A square in Imtal where the king's edicts are first delivered to the people. It has been used for coronations, funeral processions and executions.
High Province	Another of the principalities of Great Kingdom, located far to the North beyond the Borderlands. "High Province in the north—the far, far North—where amidst mountains of ice and stone the rivers boil and fill the air with blankets of fog."
High Road	Northernmost garrison town in Imtal Proper. Near the Borderlands on the Kingdom side of the Krasnyj River. "The sole purpose of the elite High Road Garrison Guardsmen is to provide travelers with safe passage along the Kingdom's High Road and to shield the Kingdom from bandit incursions out of the north."
Hindell	An independent state managed by Family Hindell. According to the 2nd Alliance, Hindell is a free nation but most of the lands have been traded back to Great Kingdom over the years.
Human Magus	A mage of the race of Man. The last Human Magus was Efryadde who perished in the Blood Wars.

I (Imson Adylton – Ispeth, Duke)

Imson Adylton	Captain Adylton. Imtal garrison captain.
Imtal	Capital of Great Kingdom. In ancient times, Imtal was the

name of a great warrior sword sworn to the Alder, first king of Great Kingdom. In the early days of the Blood Wars, Imtal by himself defended the Alder against an army of assassins. He died with his blade in his hands and is said to have taken fifty assassins with him.

Instra   City built at the mouth of Instra River in Vostok. The Old Kingdom word *inst* can mean either tool or spear depending on interpretation.

Isador Froen d'Ga   Lady Isador. Nanny for Adrina; given honorary title of Lady by King.

Ispeth   Lands of Duke Ispeth, small and swamp-infested but renowned for its apples. Ispeth and her people have been strong allies of the Great Kingdom since the time of the Alder. The apples of Ispeth are the best in the land and often grace King Andrew's table.

Ispeth, Duke   Ruler of the independent Duchy of Ispeth. "Duke Ispeth is not the most trusting of men. I've had the pleasure of his company on several occasions, I know. If he sees plots and spies in the passage of a mere messenger across Ispeth, who knows what he thinks seeing this mob... We'll not be traveling anymore this day."—Emel Brodstson.

J (Jacob Froen d'Ga - Jrenn)

Jacob Froen d'Ga   Father Jacob. First minister to the king. Head of the priesthood in the capital city of Imtal. (See illustration)

Jarom Tyr'anth   King Jarom, ruler of Vostok, East Warden of the Word.

Jasmin	Sister Jasmin. First priestess of the Mother.
Jeshowyn	A road named after a soothsayer who brought the city of Skunne and Pakchek to the same side. Supposedly his spirit still binds the cities together.
Joshua	Priest of the Father.
Jrenn	A floating city located along the Krasnyj River near High Road. It is a Kingdom town, hidden away within the Mouth of the World. Jrenn was previously home to the royal fleet of Oshywon.

K (Kastelle – Ky'el)

Kastelle	A swamp northwest of Beyet. In ancient Greye, Kastelle was a lord and the lover of Adrynne who was a traitor to the king of Shost. It is said the swamp maintains a narrow finger so the two may always touch, even during times of droughts. The two swamps forever protect the city of Beyet's west side.
Keeper	See Lore Keepers.
Keeper Martin	See Martin Braddabaggon.
Keille Tae	Son of Ashwar.
Khennet	Village under protection of Damen.
King Cat Patrol	Legendary defenders of Gregortonn. They ride enormous tigers called king's cats. Few have survived encounters with a king cat in the wild. King cats are fiercely independent but once they bond with their rider, it's a bond that cannot be broken.
Kingdom Alliance	A peace accord signed by Great Kingdom, Vostok, Sever, Zapad and Yug to end the Blood Wars. Also called the Alliance of Kingdoms.
Kingdom of the Sky	A reference to the Dragon kingdoms of old, lost like the Dragon's Keep in the mists of time.
King's Mate	An ancient game played by soldiers and scholars.
Klaive	Small barony in South Province that is rich in resources. Home of renowned shipwrights.

One of the Great Houses. Family Klaive is headed by Baron Michal Klaive.

Klaive Keep Knights   Skilled swordsmen and riders, renowned and feared throughout the Kingdoms.

Krasnyj River   River that flows from the Lost Lands to the West Deep. The river's depth changes dramatically with the seasons and is mostly rocky and shallow. The river's name comes from the Old Kingdom word *kras* (red) as the river is said to bleed in spring.

Krepost'   Walled city in the Western Territories. "Beyond Zashchita lay Krepost' and her ferryman who took travelers across River Krepost' so they could begin the climb into the mountain city and where afterward the gatekeeper may or may not chase them over the cliffs into Statter's Bay and to their deaths." – Jacob Krepost', *Territory Writings*

Jacob Krepost' was ordered into exile by King Enry Alder in 284 KA. It is said that the territory wildmen burned the first settlement to the ground and the only escape for Jacob and his men was to dive to their deaths into Statter's Bay.

Ky'el   Legendary titan who gave men, elves and dwarves their freedom at the dawn of the First Age.

L (Lady of the Forest – Lyudr)

Lady of the Forest   Mysterious woman who helped Adrina and told her she would find help in a most unlikely source. She is of a race unknown and the history of her people is unrecorded.

Lady of the Night   See Lady of the Forest.

Leklorall   Kapital, the capital city of East Reach. Home of the Brotherhood of Elves and Queen Mother of East Reach.

Lillath Tabborrath   Mother of Vilmos.

Liyan, Brother   Elf, presiding member of East Reach High Council.

Lore Keepers   Lore Keepers are the guardians of knowledge and history. Throughout the ages, it has been their task to record history, a mandate written by the First Keeper, known as The Law of the Lore, has kept them independent from any kingdom and outside the control of kings and queens. Their ability to communicate over long distances using dream messages is their true value, though, and the reason few kings want to risk the wrath of the Council of Keepers.

Lost Lands Uncharted lands north of Statter's Bay. According to Territory lore, these lands once belonged to a great kingdom that was swallowed by the Endless Ice.

Lower Council The people's council of Great Kingdom. Handles affairs of local areas and outlying provinces, including land disputes and tax collection.

Lycya Kingdom swallowed by the desert during the Race Wars; now known as the Barrens.

Lyudr Hills at the western edge of the Samguinne Mountains. In ancient Greye, a bandit lord who was the first to discover paths through the hills to Oshio. He led numerous raids into Oshio.

M (Marek - Myrial)

Marek A walled city of Damen. Noble families: Icthess, Teprium. Lords: Ryajek, Ittwar.

Mark, King The Elven King of West Reach. (See illustration)

Martin Braddabaggon Keeper Martin. A lore keeper and head of the Council of Keepers.

Master Engineer Field engineers are responsible for many of the dark horrors used on the battlefields of Ruin Mist. They are the builders of mobile towers, battering rams, ballista, catapults and defensive trenches. Whenever there is a long campaign, you can be sure that field engineers will be deployed along with the troops, and that the master engineer will have many resources at his disposal.

Mellack   A small holding of Great Kingdom near the Duchy of Ispeth.

One of the Great Houses. Family Mellack is headed by Elthia Mellack, Baroness of Mellack.

Michal Klaive   Baron Klaive. Low-ranking noble whose lands are rich in natural resources.

Midori   Sister Midori. The name Princess Delinna Alder earned after joining the priestesses. Her black hair, green jewel-like eyes, and high cheekbones mark her as one of noble blood and a daughter of King Andrew. Since she has been exiled from the Kingdom. (See illustration)

Mikhal   Captain Mikhal. Quashan' garrison captain.

Mir   A free city state, officially formed under the 2nd Alliance. The name is from the Old Kingdom word *mer* (soil or dirt).

Moeck   A Kingdom port town on the Dead Sea, near the Cliffs of D'Ardynne.

One of the Great Houses. Family Moeck is headed by Enry Moeck, Baron of Moeck.

Mother-Earth   The great mother. She who watches over all.

Mouth of the World	A natural river cave that cuts under the Rift Range and whose Eastern bowels provide a port safe from harsh northern winds.
Mrak, King	King of the wraiths. One of the dark minions.
Myrial	Cleaning girl who becomes Housemistress of Imtal Palace. Childhood friend of Princess Adrina Alder.

N (Naiad – Nyom)

Naiad	Fresh water spirits of ancient times.
Nameless One	He that is true evil; evil incarnate.
Neadde	The current capital city of Vostok. During the reign of King Jarom I, Lord Rickard Neadde was a Bloodrule, the last Bloodrule.
Nereid	Water-dwellers; sea spirits of ancient times.
Nesrythe	Village under protection of Shost.
Nijal Solntse	First son of Geoffrey, former day captain city garrison, Free City of Solntse.
Nikol, Brother	Elf, first of the Yellow order.
Niyomi	Beloved of Dalphan, lost in the Blood Wars.
Noman, Master	Master to Amir. Keeper of the City of the Sky.
North Reach	Lands swallowed by the 20-year snow during the Race Wars; now known as the Endless Ice.
Nyom	A mountain range east of the Efrusse River named after the founder of Nesrythe. Nyom tried to lead people to safety during the Rhylle/Armore wars.

O (Odwynne Heman – Over-Earth)

Odwynne Heman	Matriarch of Family Heman. Unofficially, a baroness, though the family no longer has the right of title.
Olev Der	2nd Captain Olev Der of the Quashan' garrison. Captain of the City Watch.
Olex	Neighboring village to Vilmos' home village of Tabborrath.

One of the three villages in their cluster.

Ontyv, Brother	Elf, first of the Black order.
Opyl	A river near Klaive in Great Kingdom. Opyl Alder was the daughter of Antwar Alder, first king of Great Kingdom. She is said to have fallen in love with King Jarom I, a love that caused her to betray her father.
Oread, Queen	Great queen; first ruler of Under-Earth gnomes.
Oshio	Capital of Damen. Noble families: Ibravor, Glorre, Clareb, Darr. War Lords: Mark, Kylaurieth, Kylauriel, Hettob.
Oshywon	King of Valeria, the unrecognized kingdom. Also refers to the twelve clans.
Over-Earth	One of the three original realms of Ruin Mist. A place of myth and legend. It is said that Over-Earth is ruled by titans, dragons and the eagle lords. The only known gate to Over-Earth was sealed at the end of the Second Age and no one henceforth has ever completed the journey there and back, though many have tried and failed.

P (Pakchek – Priests of the Father)

Pakchek	Capital city of Daren. Noble families: Fiosh, Lann, Jabell, Tanney, Lebro, Thyje. War Lords: Boets, Yuvloren, Lozzan, Ghil, Chilvr, Rhil.
Papiosse	A walled City of Shost. Noble families: Papli, Ivorij.
Parren	Keeper Parren. Member of the Council of Keepers.
Pavil Hindel	Lieutenant Pavil. A sectional commander.
Peter Eragol	Baron of Eragol, head of Family Eragol. The 17th Peter in a line that goes back to the time of the Alder.
Peter Zyin	King Peter, ruler of Zapad, West Warden of the Word.
Priestess' Of Mother-Earth	Serve the land and Mother-Earth. Handle affairs of life, birth and renewal of spirit. Retreat to Sanctuary during equinox ceremonies of autumn and spring. These same times represent the peak of their powers. The Priestess' of the Mother have no known allegiance to any kingdom. Each priestess has a rank with the highest rank

being First Priestess of the Mother. Second and Third Priestess ranks are often offices of contention and there is considerable maneuvering for favor as the second priestess is not guaranteed the highest office should the first pass on or pass her office on before her death. Priestesses are referred to as Sister. Upon earning her robes, a priestess is given a name suffix which indicates her rank and place.

Priests of the Father Serve Great Father. Handle matters of matrimony and death. They preside over the winter and Summer solstice ceremonies throughout the Kingdoms. These times represent the peak of their powers. The highest level of the priesthood is the office of King's First Minister. The office of King's First Minister in Great Kingdom is held by Father Jacob. Father Jacob is charged with ensuring the natural laws of Great Father are upheld in Great Kingdom. The insignia of his office is a white sun with outward swirling rays.

Q (Qerek – Q'yer)

Qerek Village under protection of Daren.

Quashan' Capital city of South Province. Aden Quashan' was a Bloodlord who took and then held the Cliffs of D'Ardynne in the last days of the 2nd Siege.

Queen Mother The Elven Queen. Queen of East Reach, mother of her people. (See illustration)

Q'yer Keeper Q'yer. Member of the Council of Keepers.

R (Race Wars - Ry'al, Brother)

Race Wars   The war that led to the Blood Wars. It is a murky time in history that is often confused with the time of the Blood Wars. "When only the five sons of the Alder remained in power, King Jarom the First controlled nearly all the lands from Neadde to River Ispeth. It was his Blood Soldiers that pushed the enemy back to the sea near River Opyl and he with his own bare hands that committed patricide and started the last great war."

Rain Mountain   Majestic mountain in the center of Vangar forest. The mountain is said to be the source of an ancient power but the dark stories about the Vangar keep out the curious.

Rain Stones   The stones. Stones with healing properties that come from deep within Rain Mountain. Other healing stones are known to exist.

Rapir the Black   The spurned one, once a son of Great Father. Also known as the Darkone.

Razor   Galia Tyr'anth's king cat.

Reassae   Barony. Family Reassae is one of the most highly regarded Great Houses. The family and their landkeeps held the East against First and Second Coming, invasions by Territory wildmen.

One of the Great Houses. Family Reassae is headed by Gabrylle Reassae, Baron of Reassae, and King's Hand.

Redwalker Tae   Lieutenant Tae. Also known as Redcliff. A sectional commander.

Rhylle   Broad inland plains; an ancient battle place, where the Rhylle invaders were defeated, just short of Pakchek.

Lands to the east of Greye.

Riald Fraddylwicke   Baron Fraddylwicke. Low ranking nobleman with holdings in South Province. Keeper of former gateway to South.

Rickard Neadde   The last Bloodrule. Rickard supposedly wielded two great swords, one in each hand, as he went into battle. The swords, named Fire and Fury, are said to have been over six feet in length, a size dwarfed by Rickard's reported height of nearly seven feet.

Rift Range   East-West mountain range separating High Province and the Borderlands. Ice-capped mountains of jagged black rock that climb perilously into the heavens.

Rill Akh Arr   Home to those that worship Arr. It is a source of dark magic and home of the Ever Tree, the oldest living thing in all the realms.

Rudden Klaiveson   Son of Baron Klaive. Blood relative of King Jarom on his mother's side.

Ruin Mist   World of the paths; the intertwining of Under-Earth, Over-Earth and Middle-Earth.

Ry'al, Brother   Elf, second of the Blue. Heir to Samyuehl's gift.

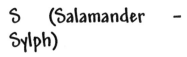

S (Salamander – Sylph)

Salamander   The fire-dwellers; lizard men of times past.

Samguinne   A mountain range dividing the Zadridos and Zabridos forests. An ancient nobleman/war lord who conducted negotiations for Greye with the Armore. Samguinne was an Armorian but served Greye.

Samyuehl, Brother   Elf, first of the Blue order.

Sathar the Dark   He that returned from the dark

journey. (See illustration)

Scarlet Hawk   Merchant ship Vilmos and Xith sailed in from Eragol to Jrenn.

Serant	Principle landholding in High Province. Also called the Lands of the North Watch. One of the Great Houses. Family Serant is headed by Edwar Serant, Governor of High Province.
Serant, Lord	See Edwar Serant.
Seth, Brother	Elf, first of the Red, protector of Queen Mother.
Sever	Smallest of the minor kingdoms.
Shalimar	A warrior of Shchander's company.
Shchander	Old compatriot of Nijal.
Shost	The 3rd kingdom of Greye.
Skunne	A walled city of Daren. Noble families: Zont, Adyir. War Lords: Zeli, Ehrgej.
Solntse	Largest of the free cities. Located on the northern edge of Great Kingdom.
Solstice Mountain	Tallest mountain in the Rift Range.
Soshi	Former love of Prince Valam Alder.
South Province	Southernmost lands of Great Kingdom. "South, beyond a forest of great white trees called giant birch, lay South Province with its capital city enveloped by the majestic Quashan' valley."
Statter's Bay	Inlet that cuts deep into the Territories and leads to Eastern Sea.
	In the Old Kingdom, a statter is the word for a dead man (from Old Kingdom *statt,* meaning still), so Statter's Bay is also called Dead Man's Bay.
Stranth	The most powerful Lord of Greye in recent times.
S'tryil, Lieutenant	See Anth S'tryil.
Stygian Palisade	Steep, rocky mountain range that cuts through the minor kingdoms.
Stytt, Sergeant	See Enry Stytt.
Sylph	Air dwellers; winged folk of times past.

T (Tabborrath - Tyr Eran)

Tabborrath   Village Vilmos was raised in; located in the Kingdom of Sever.

Taber   Ancient name for Eragol, a coastal seaport at the mouth of Krasnyj River.

Tae, Lieutenant   See Redwalker Tae.

Talem   First Priest and Ceremony Master for Priestess Council.

T'aver   Master T'aver. Elder in a small village in Fraddylwicke swamp.

Teren, Brother   Elf of the Brown.

Three Village Assembly   Each village cluster in Sever has a councilor. This councilor is a member of the assembly. Other members include the oldest living members of the village's founding families.

Timmer   Swordmaster Timmer. Swordmaster garrison at Imtal.

Trendmore, Captain   See Faryn Trendmore.

Trollbridge   River runs from Rain Mountain to West Deep.

Tsandra, Brother Elf, first of the Brown order.

Tsitadel'   Ancient stronghold of old.

Twin Sonnets   Nickname for the free cities of Mir and Veter. The Old Kingdom names, *mer* and *evet*, together refer to windblown earth, which is the common explanation for the enormous delta at the mouth of the Trollbridge River.

Two Falls   Village a day's ride north of Tabborrath.

Tyr   Klaive Knight, husband to Kautlin and father of Aryanna and Aprylle.

Tyr Eran   Lieutenant Eran, sectional commander.

U (Under-Earth - Uver)

Under-Earth   The Lands of Greye, Rhylle and Armore. The dark realm beneath the world of men.

Upper Council   The highest council of Great Kingdom. Handles issues of state, issues that pertain to all areas of the Kingdom as a whole, such as roads, garrisons and tax rates.

Uver   A region in the northern part of Greye and burial place of Uver, the founder of Greye.

V (Vadan Evgej – Vythrandyl)

Vadan Evgej   Captain Evgej. Former Swordmaster, city garrison at Quashan'.

Valam   Prince Valam. Governor of South Province. King Andrew's only son. Also known as the Lord and Prince of the South.

Valeria   Once a great kingdom of the North with holdings that stretched from Solstice Mountain to Mellack.

Vangar Forest   Great forest in the Kingdom of Sever. Many dark legends have been spun about strange beasts that hunt in the forest's shadows.

Van'te Duardin   Chancellor Van'te. Former first adviser to King Andrew, now confidant to Lord Valam in South Province.

Veter   A free city state, officially formed under the 2nd Alliance. The name is from the Old Kingdom word *evet* (air or wind).

Vilmos Tabborrath An apprentice of the forbidden arcane arts.

Vil Tabborrath   Father of Vilmos and village councilor of Tabborrath.

Voethe   A great walled city in Vostok. During the reign of the Summer King, Voethe was the capital of Vostok.

Volnej Eragol   Chancellor Volnej. High Council member, Great Kingdom.

Vostok   Largest of minor kingdoms, key piece of the four.

Vythrandyl   Village under protection of Daren.

W (Wall of the World – Wrenrandyl)

Wall of the World The Wall; North-South mountain range that separates Great Kingdom and the Territories.

Wellison   Port city in the Kingdom of Sever. Lord Geoffrey Wellison was First Knight of King Etry Riven I and is said to have fallen on a sword meant for Etry. Prince Etry, at the time, was the sole heir to the throne.

West Deep   Great western sea.

Western Reaches   Lands of King Mark.

Western Territories   Farthest holdings of Great Kingdom to the East.

Willam Ispeth   Duke Ispeth. Ruler of the independent Duchy of Ispeth.

Willam Reassae   Lieutenant Willam. A sectional commander.

William Riven   Prince William. Prince of Sever and heir to the throne.

Wolmerrelle   Shape changers, the half animal and half human race that worships Arr.

Wrenrandyl   Village under protection of Damen.

X (Xavia - Xith)

Xavia   A mystic of ancient times.

Xith   Last of Watchers, Shaman of Northern Reaches. He is most definitely a gnome though there are those that believe he is a creature of a different sort altogether. (See illustration)

Y (Yi Duardin - Ywentir)

Yi Duardin   Chancellor Yi. First adviser to King Andrew. Brother of Van'te.

Ylad', Brother   Elf, first of the White order.

Ylsa Heman   Bowman first rank. A female archer and later a sectional commander.

Y'sat	Xith's friend of old, dwells in the city of Krepost'.
Yug	Southernmost point of the known lands, one of the minor kingdoms.
Yvonne Fraddylwicke	Baroness Fraddylwicke. Low ranking noblewoman; Baron Fraddylwicke's wife.
Ywentir	Last stronghold of the Watchers; a sanctuary of old.

Z (Zapad – Zashchita)

Zapad	Minor kingdom, renowned for its wealth and the tenacity of its people.
Zashchita	A Territory city that is a defensive outpost.

The Kingdoms and the Elves of the Reaches

Don't miss this bestselling series…

**In the Service of Dragons – The sequel series to
The Kingdoms and the Elves of the Reaches**

Discover what happens when the dragons are revealed…

Dragons of the Hundred Worlds – The prequel series to
The Kingdoms and the Elves of the Reaches
Discover the time when legends were born…

Return to the Kingdoms…
Meet the guardians of the dragon realms

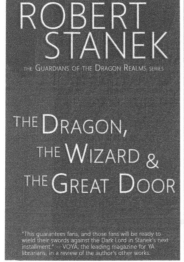 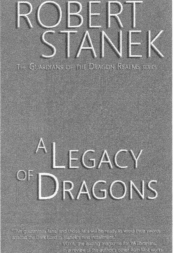